STAR WARS
DIPLOMATIC CORPS
ENTRANCE EXAM

STAR WARS UNIVERSE GUIDES AND RESOURCE MATERIALS

PUBLISHED BY BALLANTINE BOOKS

STAR WARS TECHNICAL JOURNAL

STAR WARS ENCYCLOPEDIA*

THE GUIDE TO THE STAR WARS UNIVERSE

STAR WARS: THE ESSENTIAL GUIDE TO CHARACTERS

STAR WARS: THE ESSENTIAL GUIDE TO VEHICLES AND VESSELS

STAR WARS: THE ESSENTIAL GUIDE TO WEAPONS AND TECHNOLOGY*

STAR WARS: THE ESSENTIAL GUIDE TO PLANETS AND MOONS*

STAR WARS: THE ESSENTIAL GUIDE TO DROIDS*

forthcoming

STAR WARS®

DIPLOMATIC CORPS
ENTRANCE EXAM

COMPILED BY KRISTINE KATHRYN RUSCH

OFFICE OF EMPLOYMENT RESOURCES

CORUSCANT

DEL
REY

BALLANTINE BOOKS · NEW YORK

A Del Rey® Book
Published by Ballantine Books

http://www.randomhouse.com/delrey/

Library of Congress Catalog Card Number: 97-92947

Cover design by Dreu Pennington-McNeil

Interior design by Ann Gold

Manufactured in the United States of America

First Edition: June 1997

10 9 8 7 6 5 4 3 2 1

For Kevin J. Anderson,
because he remembers what it was like long, long ago,
in a galaxy far, far away

CONTENTS

INTRODUCTION

Diplomacy is the art of the difficult. Diplomats are the glue that holds intergalactic alliances together. They are intelligent, resourceful, and heroic. Diplomats must also be knowledgeable, sensitive, and savvy.

Leia Organa Solo began acquiring these skills even before her days as the youngest Senator in the Imperial Senate. A political family adopted her, and she learned many arts of diplomacy in her childhood. When she became a leader of the New Republic, she put those diplomatic talents to use.

But diplomacy isn't for everyone, as her husband, Han Solo, is constantly reminded. Han believes there's a time for talk and a time for action. And sometimes his penchant for action hurts the delicacy of a diplomatic negotiation.

Does this mean that Han Solo can't represent the New Republic? No. What it means is that, on extremely sensitive matters, it is better to have Leia Organa do the job. She, too, believes there is a time for talk and a time for action, but she knows that words can be just as valuable as a blaster.

What you have before you is a sample exam based on the one that is given to candidates who have applied for a position with the New Republic Diplomatic Corps. Candidates must come to the corps with a minimum education in a number of subjects, including basic familiarity with galactic history, and specialized knowledge in a wide array of areas. Members of the corps, for example, may at any moment be required to know if the food they eat is poisoned, how to play the native games of a planet, and when a simple shrug means something more than "who knows?"

In addition, candidates to the Diplomatic Corps must have a working knowledge of technology. Some planets are hostile, and some are primitive. Sometimes negotiations break down, and sometimes alliances dissolve. A diplomat must be able to take action, to repair a droid or to fly an X-wing. In severe situations, a diplomat needs to know how to defuse a bomb—or create one.

Most important, a diplomat must be savvy. Diplomats need to know who the galaxy's criminals are, who the galaxy's leaders are, and who the galaxy's villains are. It would be a disaster to negotiate with the wrong representative. It might be dangerous to underestimate a planet's native.

So take the test. It touches on a broad spectrum of subjects, and utilizes material pulled from actual events that have taken place throughout galactic history. It will allow you to determine whether or not you have a position awaiting you in the Diplomatic Corps; what's more, it will help you determine what that position might be. Each question is given a point value, and there is a scoring section at the end of this booklet.

Do not be discouraged if you didn't do as well as you thought you might. This is a test that can be taken again and again. You can consult the Sources section and it will refer you to materials you can study for the next time. Eventually, you, too, will know enough to travel the galaxy as a representative of the New Republic.

Good luck.

INSTRUCTIONS

This exam is self-contained and self-administered. Within its pages are many kinds of questions, some easy and some difficult. As you proceed, keep in mind these tips:

- Multiple choice questions may have more than one answer.
- For questions that require a written answer, you are to write no more than one sentence.
- There are trick questions. A Diplomatic Corps member should expect as much in day-to-day activity.

SCORING

As you complete the test, you must keep track of your answers on a separate sheet of paper. Once you have finished the test, go to the back of the book—there you will find the correct answers. Next to each correct answer there will be a point value—add up your total based on all of the questions you answered correctly. Since the result of your scoring will be pivotal to your career placement, keep careful track as you tally the total number of points you scored. *Don't exaggerate—it won't do you any good to apply for a job you cannot successfully complete!* Then proceed to the Scoring section, where you will find a list of positions within the New Republic Diplomatic Corps.

Your score will help you to find your proper entry level within the corps. Once you have begun your career, you will find many opportunities to increase and enhance your knowledge and abilities. From there, as far as you are concerned, the stars are the limit.

HISTORY

EVENTS

1. When Darth Vader boarded her ship, Princess Leia hid the Death Star plans in:
   a. her hair
   b. Artoo-Detoo
   c. an escape pod

2. After leaving Cloud City, who left to search for Boba Fett?
   a. Lando
   b. Chewbacca
   c. Luke
   d. Princess Leia

3. Admiral Ackbar was once a slave to:
   a. Grand Moff Tarkin
   b. Darth Vader
   c. Emperor Palpatine

4. Before he joined the Rebellion, Biggs Darklighter signed on as third mate on the starship:
   a. *Rand Ecliptic*
   b. *Scardia Voyager*
   c. *Tydirium*

5. Who flew the *Millennium Falcon* in the Battle of Endor?
   a. Chewbacca
   b. Han Solo
   c. Lando Calrissian
   d. Luke Skywalker

6. TRUE OR FALSE: See-Threepio once worked as translator for Captain Antilles.

7. Who were the two Ewoks who accompanied Han, Leia, Chewie, and the two droids to the shield generator?
   a. Wicket W. Warrick
   b. Logray
   c. Chief Chirpa
   d. Paploo

8. Who fired the shot that destroyed the second Death Star?
    a. Luke Skywalker
    b. Wedge Antilles
    c. Biggs Darklighter
    d. Lando Calrissian
    e. Han Solo
    f. Leia Organa

9. Ewoks first captured Han, Luke, Chewbacca, Artoo-Detoo, and See-Threepio:
    a. using spears
    b. by stealing their blasters
    c. with Leia's help
    d. using a net/trap

10. The founder of the Rebel Alliance is:
    a. Mon Mothma
    b. Leia Organa
    c. Bail Organa
    d. Biggs Darklighter

11. When General Rieekan picked up an Imperial probe droid, it was in zone:
    a. 66
    b. 12
    c. 3

12. In the Battle of Hoth, Wedge Antilles flew as:
    a. Rogue Three
    b. Rogue Eight
    c. Rogue Two

13. When it arrived on Cloud City, the *Millennium Falcon* landed on Platform:
    a. 327
    b. 237
    c. 732

    d. 273

    e. 372

    f. 723

14. Who was Boushh?

    a. Han Solo

    b. Princess Leia

    c. Luke Skywalker

    d. an Ubese bounty hunter

15. Dash Rendar:

    a. was Gold Leader in the Battle of Yavin

    b. took down an Imperial walker in the Battle of Hoth

    c. helped rescue Han Solo from Jabba the Hutt's palace

16. Luke Skywalker's gunner Dack died:

    a. when he was hit by weapon's fire from Darth Vader's TIE fighter near the Death Star

    b. in hand-to-hand combat on the Death Star

    c. when an AT-AT's weapon's fire hit Skywalker's snowspeeder on Hoth

17. Who pinpointed the location of the second Death Star?

    a. Artoo-Detoo

    b. Mon Mothma

    c. Admiral Ackbar

    d. Bothan spies

18. Lando Calrissian turned Han and Leia over to Darth Vader in exchange for:

    a. credits

    b. safe passage out of the Empire

    c. protection for Cloud City

    d. protection for Kessel

19. When Darth Vader tried to destroy Myoris' School, who saw the Empire's strategy in a dream?
    a. Luke Skywalker
    b. Berd
    c. Anakin Solo
    d. Mara Jade

20. In the Battle of Hoth, Luke Skywalker flew as:
    a. Rogue Two
    b. Rogue Leader
    c. Rogue Five

21. Lando Calrissian was promoted to General based on his performance in:
    a. Cloud City
    b. Jabba's palace
    c. the Battle of Taanab

22. Who was the first Ewok to make contact with the Rebel forces in the Battle of Endor?
    a. Wicket W. Warrick
    b. Logray
    c. Chief Chirpa
    d. Paploo

23. TRUE OR FALSE: Luke Skywalker sponsored Skywalker Technical Maintenance Service for young pilots on Tatooine.

24. In the Battle of Yavin, Biggs Darklighter flew as:
    a. Red Seven
    b. Red Eleven
    c. Red Three

25. In the Battle of Yavin, the first attempt to blow up the Death Star was made by:
    a. Han Solo
    b. Wedge Antilles

c. Biggs Darklighter

d. Red Leader

e. Gold Leader

26. What was the name of the stolen Imperial shuttle that brought the strike team to Endor's moon?

a. *Tydirium*

b. *Tynna*

c. *Tyrann*

27. Who was Lando's copilot in the Battle of Endor?

a. Chewbacca

b. Nien Nunb

c. Wicket

28. TRUE OR FALSE: In the Battle of Yavin, Luke Skywalker saved Biggs Darklighter's life.

29. TRUE OR FALSE: In the Battle of Yavin, Red Leader's proton torpedo hit its target.

30. Where did Luke Skywalker receive his formal Jedi training?

a. Tatooine

b. Yavin 4

c. Dagobah

31. At Jabba's palace, Luke Skywalker killed Jabba's pet:

a. bantha

b. rancor

c. droid

32. Whom did Darth Vader want to freeze in carbonite?

a. Han Solo

b. Luke Skywalker

c. Princess Leia

33. Who was the Emperor's Hand?
    a. Mara Jade
    b. Roganda Ismaren
    c. Rillao
    d. Augwynne Djo

34. What was the clearance code for Darth Vader's shuttle for its arrival at the second Death Star?
    a. ST 321
    b. ST 213
    c. ST 123
    d. Blue

35. On Tatooine, who became a victim of the Great Sarlacc?
    a. Bib Fortuna
    b. Oola
    c. Salacious Crumb
    d. Boba Fett

36. How did Ben Kenobi describe Darth Vader?
    a. more machine than man
    b. twisted and evil
    c. terrifying

37. Who oversaw the final stage of construction on the second Death Star?
    a. Darth Vader
    b. Moff Jerjerrod
    c. Emperor Palpatine

38. What, according to Luke Skywalker, was the Emperor's greatest weakness?
    a. his faith in his friends
    b. his overconfidence
    c. his Jedi training
    d. his age

39. The name of Darth Vader's true self was _____ .

40. TRUE OR FALSE: The Emperor was not surprised that Luke Skywalker was with the Rebels on Endor's moon.

41. Who was in charge of Darth Vader's task force before the Battle of Hoth?
    a. Admiral Ozzel
    b. General Veers
    c. Captain Piett

42. Whose idea was it to turn Luke Skywalker to the dark side?

43. List the bounty hunters hired by Darth Vader.

44. Who was the commander in charge of overseeing the construction of the second Death Star?
    a. Grand Moff Tarkin
    b. Moff Jerjerrod
    c. Captain Pellaeon

45. Who told Darth Vader that Leia Organa was his daughter?
    a. Ben Kenobi told him.
    b. He always knew.
    c. Luke Skywalker told him.
    d. He divined it from Luke's feelings.
    e. He divined it from Ben's feelings.

46. Who killed Emperor Palpatine?
    a. Luke Skywalker
    b. Han Solo
    c. Leia Organa
    d. Darth Vader

47. Who followed the *Millennium Falcon* as it flew toward Bespin?
    a. Darth Vader
    b. Grand Moff Tarkin
    c. Nil Spaar
    d. Boba Fett

48. Darth Vader called the Emperor _____ .

49. Admiral Daala was trained:
    a. by Grand Moff Tarkin
    b. at the Imperial military academy on Carida
    c. by Captain Pellaeon

50. How many times did Emperor Palpatine execute Bevel Lemelisk?
    a. one
    b. two
    c. seven
    d. thirty-five
    e. never

51. TRUE OR FALSE: Darth Vader helped the Empire hunt down and destroy the Jedi Knights.

52. Grand Moff Tarkin did not destroy Dantooine because it was:
    a. too remote to make an effective target
    b. not a Rebel base
    c. too close to Tatooine

53. How did Darth Vader know of Ben Kenobi's presence on the Death Star?
    a. Vader saw him arrive.
    b. Vader felt a tremor in the Force.
    c. Vader ran into him in a corridor.
    d. Kenobi ambushed him.

54. TRUE OR FALSE: The Emperor believed that Luke Skywalker's compassion for Darth Vader would be Skywalker's undoing.

55. Who saved Anakin Skywalker?
    a. Darth Vader
    b. Ben Kenobi
    c. Emperor Palpatine
    d. Luke Skywalker

56. TRUE OR FALSE: Darth Vader fled the second Death Star when he discovered that it was about to explode.

57. TRUE OR FALSE: Darth Vader killed Luke Skywalker's father.

58. Why did Darth Vader let the *Falcon* escape the first Death Star?
    a. He didn't; they fought their way out.
    b. He didn't want his son to die.
    c. He placed a homing beacon on the ship.

59. In the Battle of Yavin, Darth Vader was about to shoot Luke Skywalker's X-wing when:
    a. the Death Star exploded
    b. Wedge Antilles shot Vader's wingman
    c. Han Solo shot Vader's wingman

60. TRUE OR FALSE: The first time Han Solo ever saw Princess Leia was aboard the Death Star while they were under attack by stormtroopers.

FAMOUS QUOTES

Write the name of each person who said the famous quotes below. Each question has only one answer.

1. "Help me, Obi-Wan Kenobi. You're my only hope."

2. "Wars not make one great."

3. "Strike me down with all your hatred, and your journey toward the dark side will be complete."

4. "I felt a great disturbance in the Force . . . as if millions of voices suddenly cried out in terror and were suddenly silenced."

5. "The son of Skywalker must not become a Jedi."

6. "You may have been a good smuggler, but now you're bantha fodder."

7. "The Force runs strong in your family."

8. "It's against my programming to impersonate a deity."

9. "May the Force be with us."

10. "The ability to destroy a planet is insignificant next to the power of the Force."

11. "Try not. Do. Or do not. There is no try."

12. "Traveling through hyperspace isn't like dusting crops, boy."

13. "Who's the more foolish . . . the fool or the fool who follows him?"

14. "Somebody has to save our skins."

15. "Always in motion is the future."

16. "Hokey religions and ancient weapons are no match for a good blaster at your side, kid."

17. "If you strike me down, I shall become more powerful than you can possibly imagine."

18. "The Jedi are extinct. Their fire has gone out of the universe."

19. "When I left you, I was but the learner; now I am the master."

PEOPLE

1. Who located Leia in her cell on the Death Star?
   a. Obi-Wan Kenobi
   b. Threepio
   c. Han Solo
   d. Luke Skywalker
   e. Artoo-Detoo

2. Why didn't Darth Vader know Leia was his daughter?
   a. She kept her identity hidden from him.
   b. She didn't know.
   c. She was hidden from him before her birth.

3. Who befriended Leia on Endor's moon when she crash-landed her speeder bike?
   a. a stormtrooper
   b. a Bothan
   c. an Ewok

4. Leia got her first lightsaber:
   a. by making it herself
   b. from her brother, Luke Skywalker
   c. from Vima-Da-Boda
   d. while she attended the Jedi Academy

5. Does Leia remember her mother?

6. Leia nearly made a political marriage with:
   a. Prince Xizor
   b. Prince Isolder
   c. Senator Garm Bel Iblis

7. One of Leia's childhood nicknames was _____ .

8. Leia engaged a children's tutor named:
   a. Ebrihim
   b. Engret
   c. Egome Fass

9. Who is Leia's father?
   a. Anakin Solo
   b. Bail Organa
   c. Darth Vader
   d. Emperor Palpatine
   e. Anakin Skywalker

10. Who told Leia Organa that she had a brother?
    a. Darth Vader
    b. Emperor Palpatine
    c. Ben Kenobi
    d. Luke Skywalker

11. On the Death Star, Leia was imprisoned on Level 5, Detention Block
    _____ .

12. The names of Leia's children are _____ .

13. What did Princess Leia say when she met Obi-Wan Kenobi?

14. One of Leia's mentors was:
    a. Biggs Darklighter
    b. Senator Behn-Kihl-Nahm
    c. M'yet Luure

15. TRUE OR FALSE: Leia has always trusted Lando Calrissian.

16. Luke Skywalker lived on Tatooine with:
    a. Obi-Wan Kenobi
    b. Owen and Beru Lars
    c. Leia Organa

17. Luke Skywalker's father is _____ .

18. On Hoth, what was Luke Skywalker's comlink code?
    a. Echo Three
    b. Echo Seven
    c. Echo One

19. Why did Luke Skywalker go to Cloud City?
    a. Yoda told him to.
    b. Leia left him a message saying she needed him.
    c. Darth Vader lured him there.
    d. He saw his friends in danger through the Force.

20. According to Yoda just before he became one with the Force, what
    did Luke Skywalker need to become a Jedi?
    a. more training
    b. to confront Darth Vader
    c. more experience

21. TRUE OR FALSE: Luke Skywalker was wrong when he said there was
    still good in Darth Vader.

22. What, according to Emperor Palpatine, was Luke Skywalker's greatest weakness?
    a. his faith in his friends
    b. his overconfidence
    c. his Jedi training
    d. his age

23. Name the three figures Luke Skywalker saw in the shadows after the Battle of Endor.

24. Who told Luke the truth about his sister?
    a. Emperor Palpatine
    b. Yoda
    c. Obi-Wan Kenobi
    d. Darth Vader

25. When Luke was attacked by the wampa on Hoth, he was:
    a. going back to base
    b. checking out a meteorite
    c. doing a spot check of the area outside the base

26. Luke believed his father:
    a. was a Jedi Knight
    b. served in the Clone Wars
    c. was a navigator on a spice freighter

27. In his lightsaber duel with Darth Vader in Cloud City, Luke lost his _____ .

28. After hearing Leia Organa's message, Luke agreed to go with Obi-Wan Kenobi to:
    a. Alderaan
    b. Yavin 4
    c. the Death Star
    d. Anchorhead
    e. Mos Eisley

29. Of Luke's father, Obi-Wan Kenobi said:
    a. he was the best starfighter pilot in the galaxy
    b. he was a good friend
    c. Darth Vader betrayed and murdered him
    d. All of the above
    e. None of the above

30. How did Luke Skywalker get captured in the Battle of Endor?

31. From the following list, which of Luke Skywalker's students turned to the dark side?
    a. Brakiss
    b. Dolph
    c. Lobacca
    d. Jacen Solo

32. The love of Luke Skywalker's life was:
    a. Mara Jade
    b. Callista
    c. Gaeriel

33. Han Solo told Obi-Wan Kenobi that the *Millennium Falcon* made the Kessel run in less than:
    a. 5 parsecs
    b. 12 parsecs
    c. 20 parsecs

34. On Hoth, what was Han's comlink code?
    a. Echo Three
    b. Echo Seven
    c. Echo One

35. The planet Han won in a sabacc game was:
    a. Hapes
    b. Dathomir
    c. Bakura

36. Han saved Shug Ninx when Ninx:
    a. blasted Jabba the Hutt

b. got caught running ion triggers to the Zyggurats

c. accused Lando of cheating at sabacc

37. Han wanted to name his youngest son:
    a. Luke
    b. Lando
    c. Han Solo, Jr.

38. Who took Han's frozen body off Cloud City?
    a. Lando Calrissian
    b. Boba Fett
    c. Darth Vader
    d. Jabba the Hutt

39. The languages Han Solo speaks include:
    a. Huttese
    b. Wookiee-speak
    c. Ubese

40. Who told Han that Luke and Leia were brother and sister?
    a. Luke
    b. Leia
    c. Darth Vader
    d. Obi-Wan Kenobi

41. Han has a cousin named _____ .

42. Han agreed to fly Obi-Wan Kenobi and Luke Skywalker to Alderaan for:
    a. ten thousand credits, in advance
    b. two thousand credits
    c. seventeen thousand credits

43. Before he arrived on Hoth, Han ran into a bounty hunter:
    a. on Coruscant
    b. on Yavin 4
    c. on Ord Mantell
    d. in Smuggler's Run

44. When the shield doors closed on Hoth, locking Han and Luke out, Artoo-Detoo said their chances of survival were:
    a. two to one
    b. 775 to one
    c. one million to one

45. Han Solo agreed to meet Obi-Wan Kenobi and Luke Skywalker at Docking Bay:
    a. 94
    b. 49
    c. 4-9
    d. 9-4

46. How did the *Millennium Falcon* get on the Death Star?
    a. It snuck in with the garbage.
    b. It was pulled in by a tractor beam.
    c. It was flown in through a flaw in the Death Star's design.

47. Who put a death mark on Han Solo's head?
    a. Greedo
    b. Boba Fett
    c. Jabba the Hutt
    d. Darth Vader

48. When Han, Chewie, Luke, and Obi-Wan Kenobi arrived on the Death Star they hid:
    a. in the *Falcon*'s smuggling compartments
    b. under the seats
    c. in stolen stormtrooper uniforms

49. In order to get Han Solo to help find Princess Leia, Luke Skywalker told him that:
    a. he'd be a hero
    b. there was a reward
    c. she wasn't married

50. During the rescue attempt on the Death Star, when Han, Luke, and Leia were on their way to the *Falcon* and meet up with stormtroopers, Han:
    a. shoved them all into the ship
    b. hid in a corridor
    c. chased the troopers, screaming and firing his blaster

51. When Han Solo went searching for Luke Skywalker on Hoth, he took a tauntaun because:
    a. Luke was on a tauntaun
    b. that's the only way to get around on Hoth
    c. it was too dark to take a speeder
    d. the speeders were having trouble adjusting to the cold

52. When Luke Skywalker met Chewbacca, the Wookiee was:
    a. two hundred years old
    b. an Imperial slave
    c. pilot of a smuggler's vessel

53. Chewbacca didn't want to go into the garbage chute on the Death Star because he:
    a. saw another way out
    b. knew about the monster inside
    c. knew it was a garbage masher
    d. didn't like the smell

54. In the junk room on Cloud City, Chewbacca found:
    a. Darth Vader
    b. Boba Fett
    c. See-Threepio
    d. Artoo-Detoo

55. Chewbacca owes a life debt to Han Solo because:
    a. Han saved him from stormtroopers
    b. Han saved his family from stormtroopers
    c. Han saved him from slavery

56. When Boushh asked for the bounty on Chewbacca, Jabba the Hutt initially offered:
    a. twenty-five thousand
    b. thirty-five thousand
    c. fifty thousand

57. What's the name of Chewbacca's son?
    a. Lowbacca
    b. Lumpawarump
    c. Chewbacca, Jr.

58. One of the first times Leia Organa saw Chewbacca, she:
    a. thanked him for rescuing her
    b. screamed
    c. shot him with a blaster
    d. called him a big walking carpet

59. TRUE OR FALSE: Chewbacca was Han Solo's first Wookiee friend.

60. When Chewbacca was captured by the Ewoks, he was:
    a. bound by vines and carried on a pole
    b. wrapped in chains
    c. led into the village at spear point
    d. carried into the village on a litter

61. The name of Chewbacca's homeworld is:
    a. Wookiee
    b. Kasarax
    c. Kashyyyk
    d. Wooshyyk

62. When Obi-Wan Kenobi saved Luke Skywalker from the Sand People, he:
    a. had the help of Artoo-Detoo
    b. killed five with his lightsaber
    c. terrified them with a great howling moan

63. On Tatooine, Obi-Wan Kenobi was known as _____ .

64. Leia Organa asked Obi-Wan Kenobi to bring the Death Star plans to:
    a. the Rebel base in Yavin 4
    b. her ship, *Alderaan*
    c. Alderaan
    d. Coruscant

65. When Darth Vader met Obi-Wan on the Death Star, he said:
    a. "The circle is now complete."
    b. "You can't win."
    c. "You will die, old man."

66. In his duel with Darth Vader, Obi-Wan lifts his lightsaber out of the fight when:
    a. he knows he has lost
    b. Vader seduces him to the dark side
    c. he sees Luke Skywalker

67. Why didn't Obi-Wan tell Luke the truth about his father?
    a. he did, from a certain point of view
    b. because he felt Luke couldn't handle the information
    c. because he didn't know the truth

68. What did Obi-Wan Kenobi call Anakin Skywalker?
    a. weak
    b. a good friend
    c. twisted and evil

69. When Luke visits Obi-Wan in his home, Obi-Wan gives Luke a gift. It is:
    a. a chest
    b. a landspeeder
    c. Artoo-Detoo
    d. a lightsaber

70. What two things clued Obi-Wan Kenobi to the fact that stormtroopers, not Sand People, killed the Jawas?

71. Owen Lars bought See-Threepio because:
    a. he needed a protocol droid
    b. Threepio and Artoo-Detoo were a package deal
    c. Threepio knew Bocce

72. TRUE OR FALSE: Darth Vader shot Artoo-Detoo in the Battle of Yavin.

73. Upon arrival on Dagobah, Artoo-Detoo:
    a. found Yoda
    b. watched the X-wing sink into a bog
    c. lost his balance and fell into a boggy swamp

74. What did See-Threepio see on Cloud City that got him tossed in the junk heap?
    a. Darth Vader
    b. stormtroopers
    c. another protocol droid

75. When See-Threepio and Artoo-Detoo first saw Jabba the Hutt, Artoo:
    a. attempted to use a computer to determine the location of Lando and Chewbacca
    b. attempted to release Han Solo
    c. played a message from Luke Skywalker offering Artoo and Threepio to Jabba as gifts
    d. refused to communicate with Jabba

76. When the Ewoks first saw See-Threepio they:
    a. were terrified of him
    b. tried to kill him
    c. thought he was a god

77. When Luke Skywalker first worked on Artoo-Detoo, he accidentally started a hologram of:
    a. the Death Star
    b. Princess Leia
    c. the capture of the Rebel ship

78. When Han Solo landed the *Falcon* in what he thought was an asteroid cave, he had See-Threepio:
    a. scout the interior of the cave for mynocks
    b. talk to the *Falcon* to find out what was wrong with the hyperdrive
    c. guard the cockpit

79. Artoo-Detoo's duties on Jabba the Hutt's sail barge were:
    a. to keep the repulsorlifts running
    b. to work the computerized doors
    c. to serve drinks

80. What did Jabba the Hutt do with the protocol droid he had before See-Threepio?
    a. disintegrated him
    b. dismembered him
    c. wiped his memory

81. At an Ewok banquet in Threepio's honor, what was to be the main course?
    a. wild berries
    b. a stormtrooper
    c. Han Solo

82. How did Threepio convince the Ewoks to adopt the others into the tribe?
    a. by ordering them to do so
    b. by "magic"
    c. by including them in the story of the Galactic Civil War

83. When See-Threepio communicated with the *Millennium Falcon* after the Battle of Hoth, he:
    a. thought it spoke in an unusual dialect
    b. learned that the power coupling on the positive access had been polarized
    c. needed Artoo-Detoo to translate

84. Who convinced the Ewoks that Threepio had "magical" abilities?
    a. Leia
    b. Chewbacca
    c. Luke

85. When Artoo left the Lars Homestead, he:
    a. went to Yavin 4
    b. went to Obi-Wan Kenobi
    c. was captured by Jawas

86. TRUE OR FALSE: Artoo-Detoo understands Basic.

87. TRUE OR FALSE: When Anakin Solo went to the Jedi academy, he took Threepio with him.

88. On Telti, Artoo:
    a. led a troop of astromech droids to the control center
    b. waited for Cole Fardreamer to find Brakiss
    c. landed Luke's X-wing

89. When Artoo-Detoo and See-Threepio were sent to the Kalarba system, in the years before they knew Princess Leia and Luke Skywalker, they went because:
    a. Han Solo commanded it
    b. they were sold sight unseen to a junk trader
    c. they were on a peace mission

90. The guardians of peace and justice in the Old Republic were _____.

91. Who started the Shadow Academy?
    a. Nil Spaar
    b. Roganda Ismaren
    c. Brakiss
    d. Kueller

92. The Ssi-ruuk are:
    a. Imperial guards
    b. invaders from an outside galaxy
    c. guardians of the Katana fleet

93. Hethrir:
    a. was appointed by Darth Vader as Procurator of Justice
    b. kidnapped the Solo children
    c. defeated Luke Skywalker in a lightsaber battle

94. Who heads the Human League?
    a. Nichos Marr
    b. Gallandro
    c. Jan Dodonna
    d. Thracken Sal-Solo

THE JEDI KNIGHTS

LORE, THEORY, AND THE FORCE

TRUE OR FALSE:

1. Jedi can go into a trance that will lower their metabolism.
2. Jedi can feel the Force flowing through them.
3. Jedi cannot use the Force to pull weapons to them.
4. A Jedi's size has no correlation to a Jedi's abilities.
5. Jedi dream in hibernation trances.
6. The Force is what gives the Jedi power.

7. A single ysalamiri can:
   a. kill a Jedi Knight
   b. create a bubble in which the Force does not exist
   c. cause the Force to double in power

8. Anger, fear, and aggression:
   a. cancel out the Force
   b. lead to the dark side
   c. can be controlled through the Force

9. The Nightsisters of Dathomir are also known as:
   a. the Dathomir Jedi
   b. the witches of Dathomir
   c. the Dathomir Knights

10. The Force is _____ created by all living things.

11. The Force:
    a. obeys your commands
    b. controls your actions
    c. changes your personality

12. TRUE OR FALSE: The Force is a lot of simple tricks.

13. The dark side is:
    a. more exciting
    b. easier
    c. quicker
    d. more seductive

14. TRUE OR FALSE: To use the Force you must let go of your conscious self and act on instinct.

15. Who of those listed below were seduced by the dark side of the Force?
    a. Ben Kenobi
    b. Emperor Palpatine
    c. Luke Skywalker
    d. Anakin Solo
    e. Anakin Skywalker
    f. Yoda
    g. Leia Organa Solo
    h. Exar Kun
    i. Jorus C'baoth

16. TRUE OR FALSE: The Force can have a strong influence on the weak-minded.

17. An animal that attacks Force users is:
    a. ysalamiri
    b. vornskr
    c. womp rat

18. Luke Skywalker learned how to make his lightsaber from:
    a. Obi-Wan Kenobi
    b. a book given him by Yoda
    c. Yoda
    d. a book he found at Obi-Wan Kenobi's house

TRUE OR FALSE:
19. A lightsaber *must* have three focusing jewels.
20. Jedi Holocrons are sensitive to the Force.
21. A Jedi craves adventure and excitement.
22. A Jedi uses the Force for knowledge and defense, never for attack.
23. Teachings in Jedi Holocrons may be accessed by anyone.
24. A Jedi Knight can feel great disturbances in the Force.

JEDI HISTORY

1. Boda Baas was a Jedi who:
    a. lived in the Adega system
    b. trained Ben Kenobi
    c. turned to the dark side

2. The first Dark Lord of the Sith was:
    a. Darth Vader
    b. Jorus C'baoth
    c. Exar Kun

3. TRUE OR FALSE: Ulic Qel-Droma was stripped of his Force ability.

4. Callista's Jedi Master was:
    a. Anakin Skywalker
    b. Obi-Wan Kenobi
    c. Djinn Altis

5. TRUE OR FALSE: Luke Skywalker first heard Ben Kenobi's ghostly voice as Luke was about to fire proton torpedoes into the Death Star.

6. Dark Jedi are:
    a. Jedi who cannot survive the cave on Dagobah
    b. a vision of the reborn Emperor: Jedi Knights trained under the dark side
    c. evil Jedi Knights who operated the trench guns on the Death Star
    d. a group of evil Jedi who threatened the Bpfassh system

7. When Luke Skywalker saw Obi-Wan Kenobi on Hoth, Obi-Wan told him:
    a. that Han Solo was coming
    b. to go to the Dagobah System
    c. that Luke will not die
    d. that Luke must trust the Force

8. How many years did Yoda teach Jedi?
    a. 100
    b. 800
    c. 900

9. Whose words inspired Luke Skywalker to start the Jedi academy?

10. What were those words?

11. Darth Vader was an easy target for the dark side because:
    a. Vader was basically evil
    b. Ben Kenobi thought he could teach as well as Yoda did
    c. the Emperor brainwashed Vader

12. TRUE OR FALSE: The cave at Dagobah contained a cylinder left by a Dark Jedi.

13. From the list below, choose the names of those who sat on the Alliance High Command when Luke Skywalker proposed the Jedi academy:
    a. Jan Dodonna
    b. Borsk Fey'lya
    c. Voren Na'al
    d. Carlist Rieekan
    e. Crix Madine
    f. Admiral Ackbar
    g. Spero
    h. Wedge Antilles
    i. Garm Bel Iblis
    j. Admiral Drayson

14. When Callista left the *Eye of Palpatine*, she did so in:
    a. the computer
    b. Cray's body
    c. Nichos' body

15. The spirit of Exar Kun was defeated by:
    a. the power of Luke Skywalker
    b. the joined talents of the Jedi academy students
    c. Jacen and Jaina Solo
    d. the ghosts of Yoda and Obi-Wan Kenobi

16. Dorsk 81 died when he:
    a. went over to the dark side

b. let the combined Force from the other Jedi students help him displace seventeen Star Destroyers

c. tried to stop the bombing of the clone factory on Khomm

17. Joruus C'baoth was:
    a. a Jedi Master in the Old Republic
    b. a clone
    c. one of six Jedi Masters on the Outbound Flight Project

18. How old was Yoda when he died?
    a. 100
    b. 800
    c. 900

Match the original students of the Jedi academy with the skills that initially showed their abilities in the Force:

19. Gantoris
20. Streen
21. Kyp Durron
22. Kirana Ti
23. Dorsk 81
24. Kam Solusar

    a. could sense impending earthquakes on Eol Sha
    b. son of a Jedi, had lived in self-imposed exile to avoid the dark side
    c. a Force-wielding witch from Dathomir
    d. taught basic Force skills by Vima-Da-Boda in the spice mines of Kessel
    e. a clone who, unlike the others he was "related to," had powers they did not
    f. a cloud prospector on Bespin who always knew when an atmospheric upheaval would happen

INTERSTELLAR TRAVEL

ASTRONOMY AND GEOGRAPHY

1. How many inhabited star systems are there?
   a. twelve
   b. twelve hundred
   c. twelve thousand
   d. twelve million
   e. twelve billion

2. The Maw, one of the wonders of the universe, is a black hole cluster. Old Republic scientists believed:
   a. that it had been built by a vastly powerful ancient race to open gateways to new dimensions
   b. probability dictated that in the universe something like the Maw had to happen once
   c. that the Maw did not exist

3. What is the distance between Myrkr and Wayland?
   a. 350 light-years
   b. 50 light-years
   c. 3,000 light-years

4. TRUE OR FALSE: Alderaan was in the Dagobah system.

5. Nkllon:
   a. orbits close to its sun
   b. is a very cold planet
   c. is in the Athega system
   d. has a slow rotation
   e. All of the above
   f. None of the above

Match these planet/moon/system names with their descriptions:

6. Vorzyd 5
7. Nar Shaddaa
8. Yavin
9. Vortex

10. Dantooine
11. Phelarion
12. Hoth
13. Ryloth
14. Bespin
15. Sullust
16. Sanctuary Moon
17. Ota
18. Umgul
19. Nal Hutta
20. Despayre
21. Tatooine
22. Dagobah
23. Alderaan
24. Corellia
25. Plawal

    a. the penal planet where the Death Star was built
    b. leading producer of megonite
    c. Gambler's World
    d. home of the Cathedral of the Winds
    e. Luke Skywalker's home planet
    f. an ice planet; sixth planet in a star system of the same name
    g. swamp planet; home of Yoda
    h. the spaceport moon that orbits Nal Hutta
    i. has ice canyons; home of the Snogar
    j. sports center; home of blob races
    k. a gas giant planet with dozens of moons
    l. a remote planet, once a base for the Rebel Alliance
    m. a Tibanna gas mining colony
    n. a dry, rocky world; home of the Twi'leks
    o. the forest moon of Endor
    p. the Rebel Alliance armada gathered here before the Battle of Endor
    q. the birthplace of Jabba the Hutt
    r. known for its fast ships, pirates, and as the birthplace of Han Solo

s. home of Leia Organa Solo; no longer exists

t. location of Platt's Well, once the hiding place for Jedi children

26. Which of the following places are on Kashyyyk?
   a. Mos Eisley
   b. Rwookrrorro
   c. Badlands
   d. Toshi Station

27. Identify items marked on the map of Tatooine.

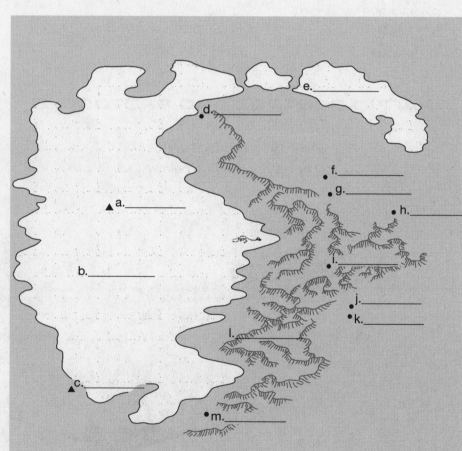

28. The spice mines are located on:
    a. Dantooine
    b. Kessel
    c. Hoth

29. The site of Echo Base is:
    a. Dantooine
    b. Kessel
    c. Hoth

30. Beggar's Canyon is on:
    a. Alderaan
    b. Corellia
    c. Tatooine

TRAFFIC CONTROL AND PROTOCOLS

SHIP IDENTIFICATION I
List name of each ship below.

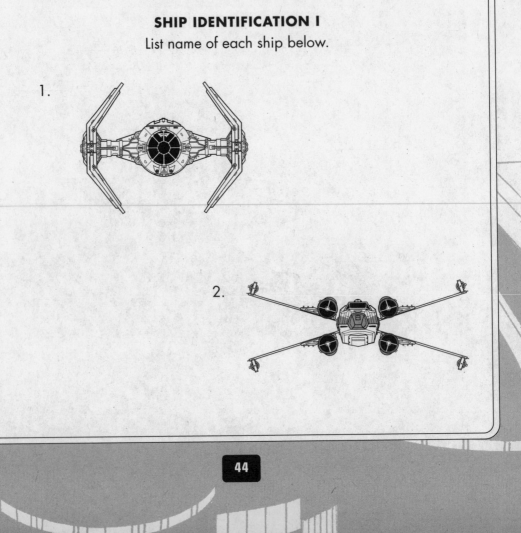

1.

2.

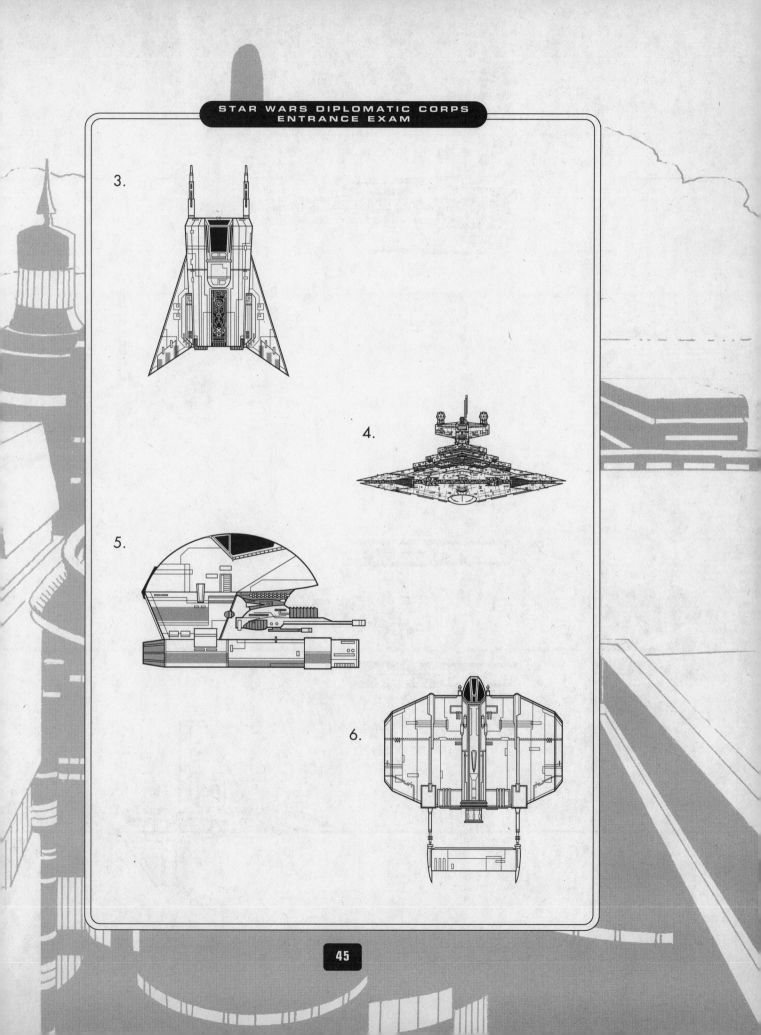

3.

4.

5.

6.

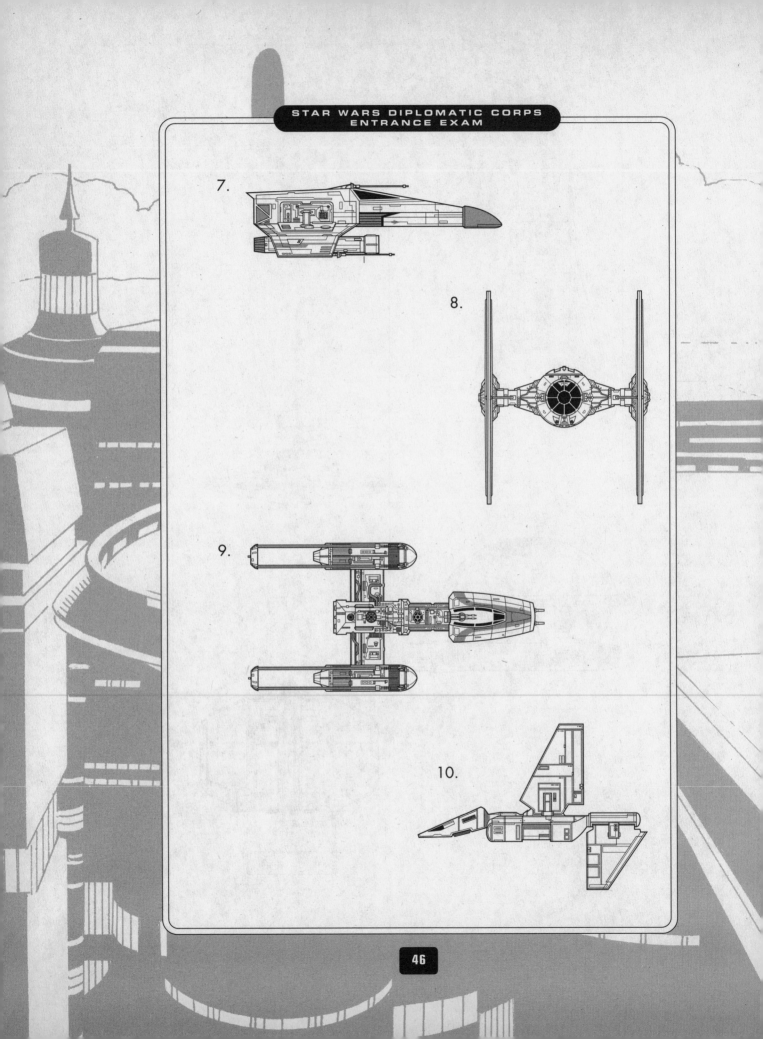

7.

8.

9.

10.

11.

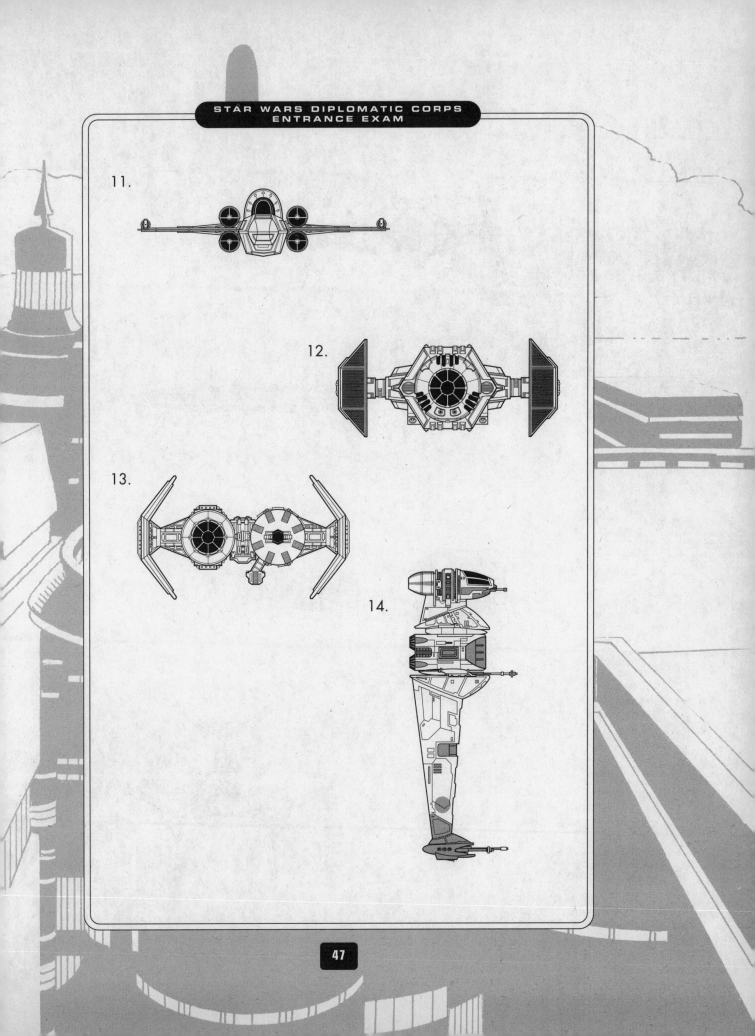

12.

13.

14.

15.

16.

17.

18.

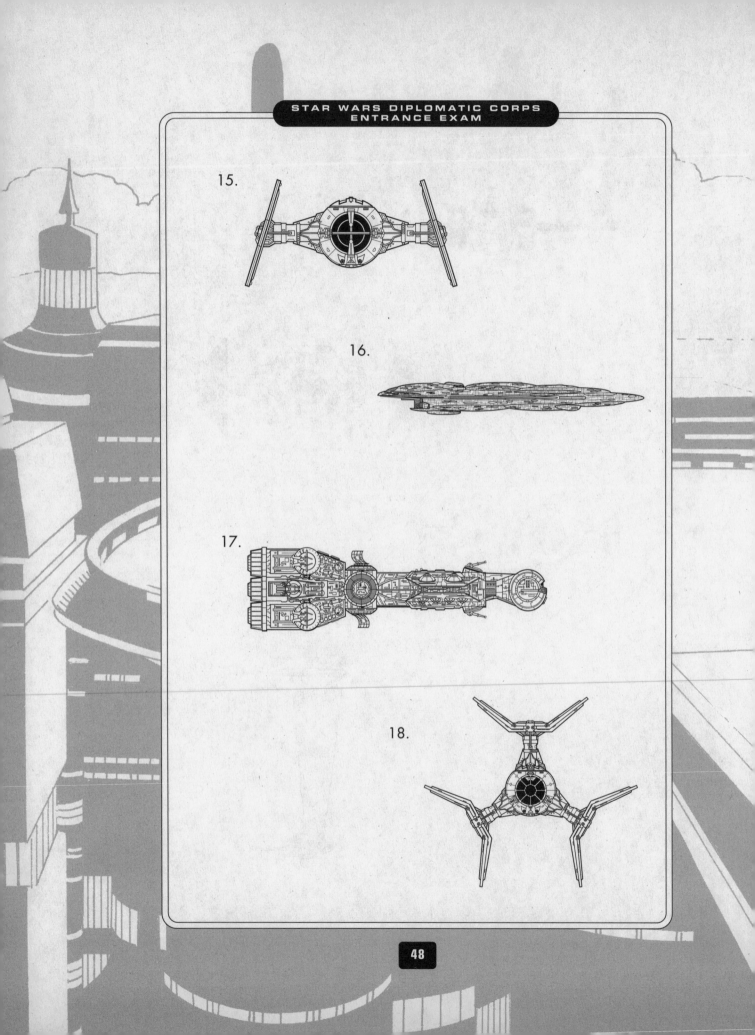

19.

20.

21.

22.

SHIP IDENTIFICATION II

Match these owners with their ships.

1. Lando Calrissian
2. Djinn Altis
3. Queen Mother Ta'a Chume
4. Mara Jade
5. Talon Karrde
6. Leia Organa Solo
7. Xizor
8. Salla Zend
9. Boba Fett
10. Admiral Daala
11. Prince Isolder
12. Dash Rendar
13. Han Solo
14. Guri
15. Grand Moff Tarkin

a. *Alderaan*
b. *Storm*
c. *Outrider*
d. *Wild Karrde*
e. *Slave II*
f. *Virago*
g. *Starlight Intruder*
h. *Millennium Falcon*
i. *Slave I*
j. *Chu'unthor*
k. *Lady Luck*
l. *Knight Hammer/Night Hammer*
m. *Star Home*
n. *Jade's Fire*
o. *Stinger*
p. The Death Star

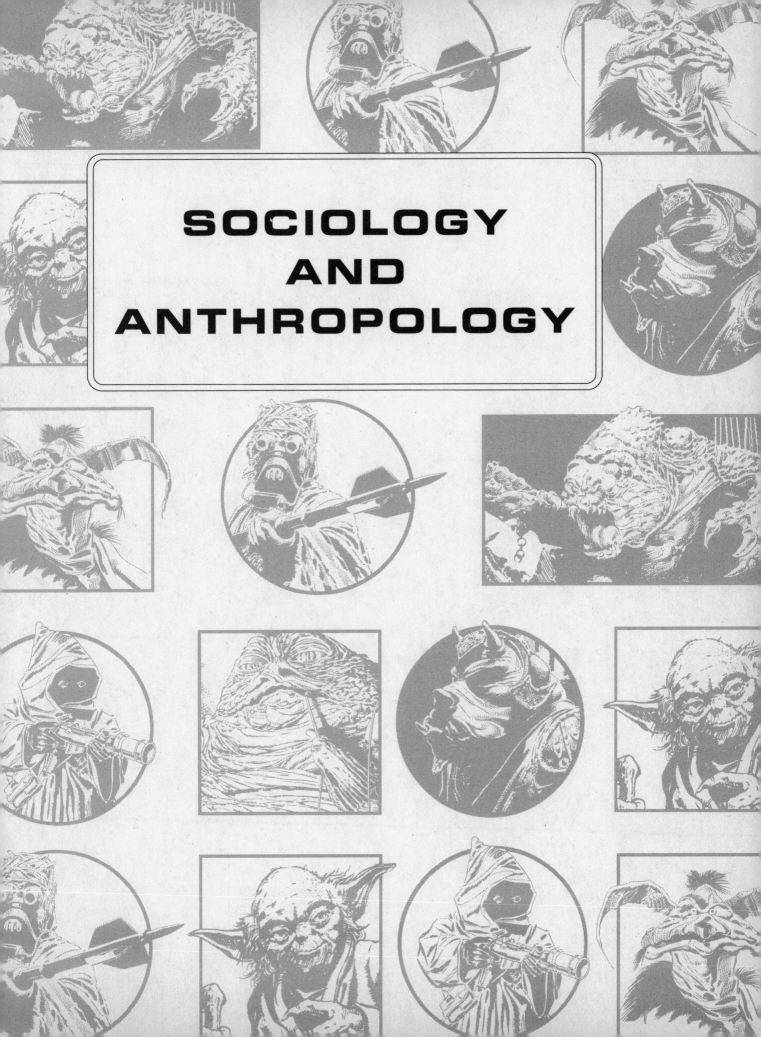

SOCIOLOGY AND ANTHROPOLOGY

POLITICAL AFFILIATIONS

Match these planets/systems/cities to their political affiliation during the Rebellion against the Empire. The places were either affiliated: (a) with the Empire, (b) with the Rebel Alliance, or (c) not affiliated. (Some questions may have more than one answer, to reflect a change in status.)

1. Kessel
2. Phelarion
3. Coruscant
4. Vorzyd 5
5. Despayre
6. Dantooine
7. Khomm
8. Wayland
9. Hoth
10. Gall
11. Eol Sha
12. Alderaan
13. Dagobah
14. Sullust
15. Bakura

16. Hapes
17. Msst
18. Bothawui
19. Carida
20. Yavin 4
21. Dathomir
22. Telti
23. Rion
24. Byss
25. Arda-2
26. Randa
27. Toprawa
28. Mos Eisley
29. Cloud City

LINGUISTICS AND LITERATURE

1. In Huttese, *Nal Hutta* means:
    a. "welcome"
    b. "destroy Hutt"
    c. "glorious jewel"

2. The Twi'lek language combines verbal components with:
    a. hand gestures
    b. whistles
    c. subtle head-tail movements

3. In Hapan, *Ereneda* means:
   a. "she who has *no* equal"
   b. "she who is strong"
   c. "she who is wise"

Match these proverbs with their country/culture of origin:

4. Predictability is comfort.

5. Even when fighting the great sabercat, it is best not to turn your back upon the lowly serpent.

6. Vengeance is like fine wine; it should be aged until perfect.
   a. Sith
   b. Falleen
   c. Khomm

7. In *The Little Lost Bantha Cub*, who reunites the lost cub with his herd?
   a. a moisture farmer
   b. a droid
   c. a krayt dragon
   d. Sand People

8. Bimms do not speak, they _____ .

9. When Gands are really mortified, they:
   a. do not speak
   b. speak of themselves in the third person
   c. refer to themselves with their family name

10. Among Bothans, names ending in "y'lya" often means:
    a. the Bothan has honor
    b. the Bothan has achieved royal status
    c. the Bothan has children

SOCIAL CUSTOMS

(These questions are specifically focused on matters of entertainment, since these are the things a diplomat *must* know.)

1. Wookiees who lose at games have been known to:
   a. pull people's arms out of their sockets
   b. destroy the playing area
   c. kill their opponent

2. Random sabacc:
   a. has five different sets of rules, shifted by chance
   b. is outlawed on Corellia
   c. is played with buttons
   d. is played by teams, the individual players shifted by chance

3. Who holds the record for winning Cosmic Chance the most times in a row?

4. The blob racing stadium on Umgul is a:
   a. round track made of permacrete
   b. hovering circle with a fourteen item obstacle course
   c. vast sinkhole collapsed into the top of a bluff
   d. multicolored plate held in the hands of gamblers

5. The suits in sabacc are _____ .

6. Fleck-eel, when dipped in boiling pepper oil, must be _____ .

7. Imported grazer must be tender and perfectly seasoned to:
   a. mix with spicy greens
   b. serve to diplomats
   c. counteract the aftertaste

8. Skip any of the 97 steps in the preparation of Moonglow, and the result could be _____ .

9. Flounut butter best compliments _____ .

10. Forvish ale can be identified by _____ .

11. A Red Dwarf must be _____ .

12. The best champagne is _____ .

13. The color of a properly prepared Orgone Bubbler is _____ .

14. Darth Vader's favorite drink was _____ .

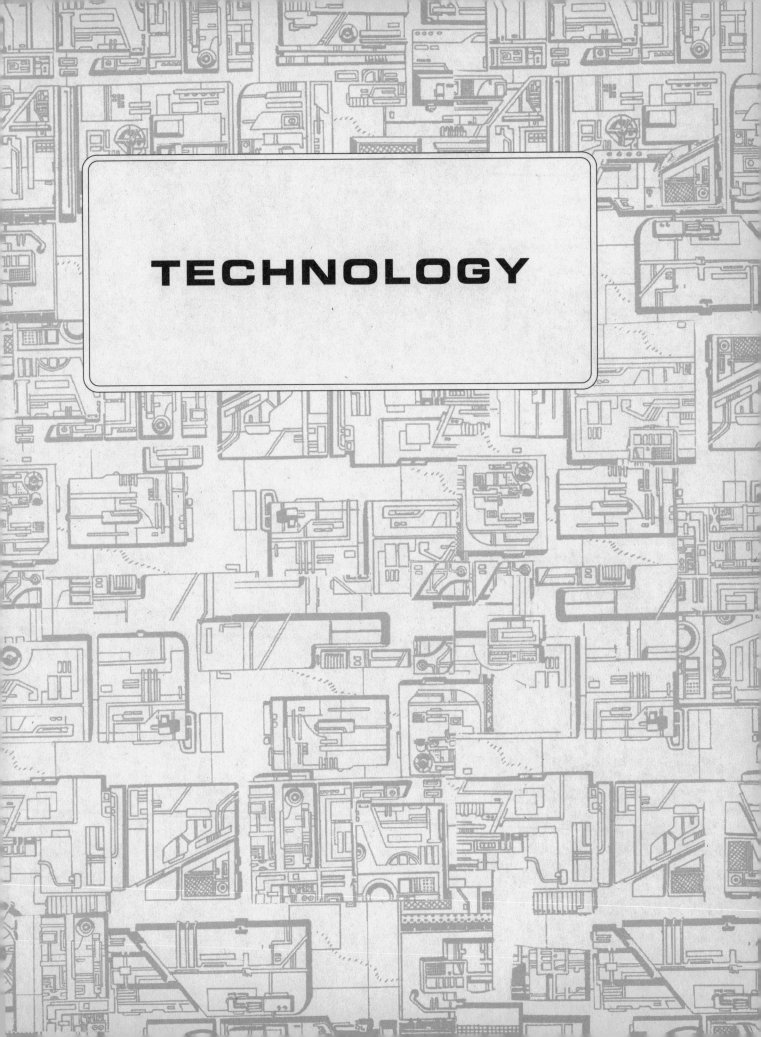

TECHNOLOGY

1. Jawas travel in what kind of vehicles:
   a. Corellian corvettes
   b. sandcrawlers
   c. swoops
   d. All of the above
   e. None of the above

2. A sail barge is propelled by:
   a. sails
   b. repulsorlifts
   c. a powerful thrust engine

3. If you nudge one energizer out of alignment in a TIE fighter:
   a. the laser cannons go off
   b. the recharge system becomes a bomb
   c. the propulsion system freezes

4. When working with a Verpine, remember that they normally count in:
   a. Base Four
   b. Base Six
   c. Base Ten

5. Droids are not allowed to enter:
   a. the Mos Eisley Cantina
   b. Hovertaxis on Corellia
   c. Skip 5 on Smuggler's Run

6. Droids visiting Bakura must:
   a. avoid bars
   b. have restraining bolts
   c. remain in the orbiting ships

7. Where is a restraining bolt located on a protocol droid?

8. TRUE OR FALSE: The binary language of moisture vaporators is similar to the language of binary loadlifters.

9. TRUE OR FALSE: Human replica droids have never been successfully implemented.

10. Enhanced nanny droids have:
    a. six arms
    b. extra soft skin for cradling babies
    c. blaster barrels hidden in each wrist

11. How many secondary functions is a protocol droid programmed for?
    a. thirty
    b. one hundred
    c. two million

12. Military protocol droids are fluent in:
    a. six million forms of communication
    b. six million forms of communication *and* an equivalent number of current and historical military doctrines, regulations, honor codes, and protocols
    c. six million forms of communication *and* an equivalent number of current and historical diplomatic doctrines, regulations, honor codes, and protocols

13. TRUE OR FALSE: Imperial probe droids are programmed to fight back when captured.

14. Protocol droids are fluent in:
    a. six million forms of communication
    b. six million forms of communication *and* an equivalent number of current and historical military doctrines, regulations, honor codes, and protocols
    c. six million forms of communication *and* an equivalent number of current and historical diplomatic doctrines, regulations, honor codes, and protocols

IDENTIFY THE PARTS
OF AN R2 ASTROMECH DROID

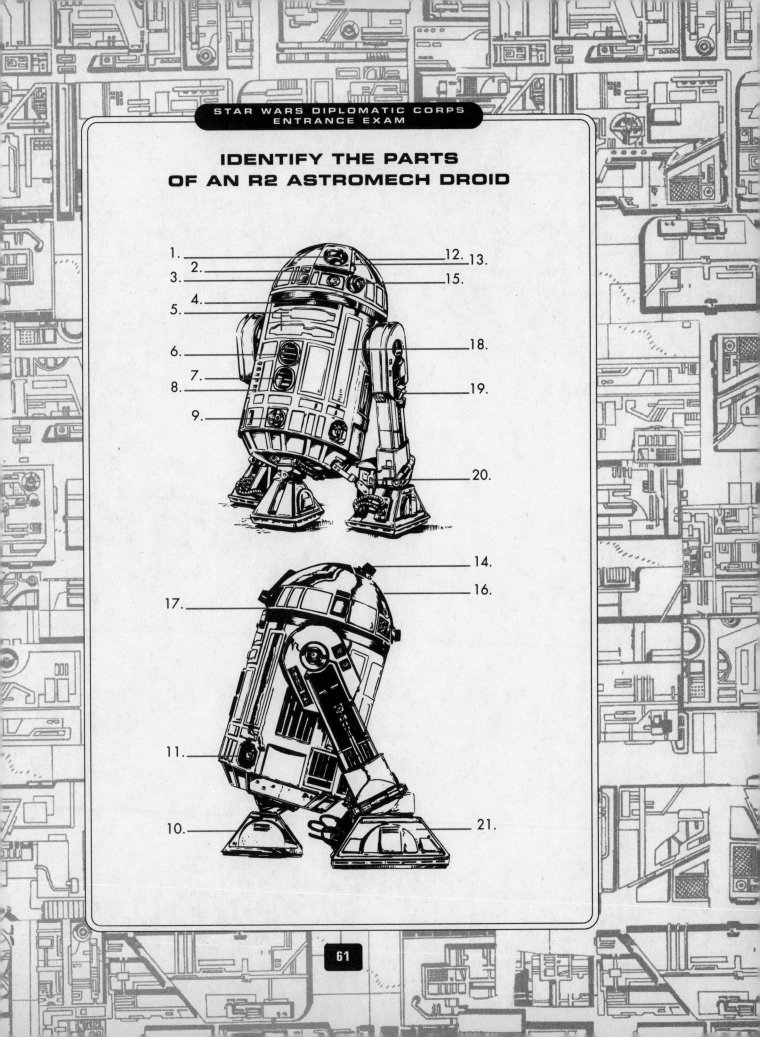

1.
2.
3.
4.
5.
6.
7.
8.
9.
12. 13.
15.
18.
19.
20.

14.
16.
17.
11.
10.
21.

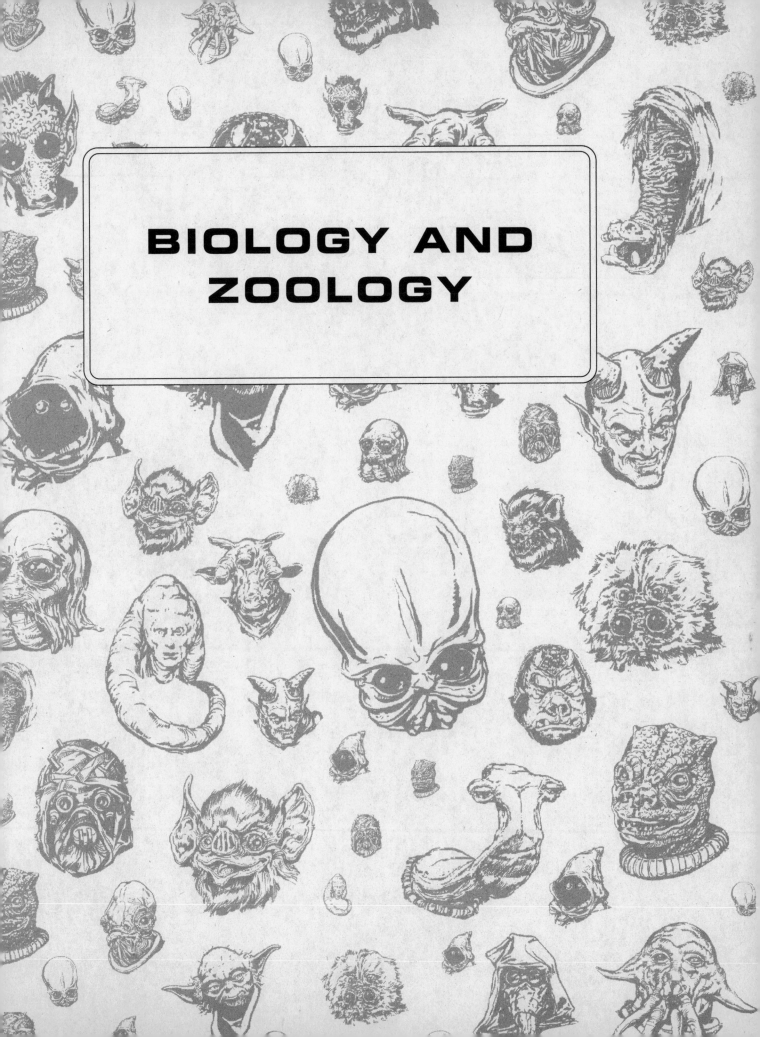

BIOLOGY AND ZOOLOGY

1. Ewoks are:
   a. fierce warriors
   b. hunter-gatherers
   c. cave dwellers

2. Piranha beetles are native to _____ .

3. Vornskrs hunt in the _____ .

4. Tauntauns are native to _____ .

5. Tusken Raiders have a mental bonding with their _____ .

6. Mynocks feed on _____ .

7. Ewoks are found:
   a. on Endor
   b. on Endor's moon
   c. in the Endor system

8. It takes the Sarlacc _____ to digest his food.

9. Rybet fingers are long and wide at the end, showing signs of vestigial _____ .

10. Wampas:
    a. are native to Wayland
    b. hunt when they're hungry
    c. never capture live prey
    d. stand out in their environment because of their white fur
    e. All of the above
    f. None of the above

11. Space slugs live in _____ .

12. Mistmakers _____ their victims before killing them.

13. Before the Battle of Endor, the only known specimen of a rancor existed:
    a. on Hoth
    b. in Nandreeson's lair
    c. in Jabba the Hutt's palace

14. Hawk-bats prey on _____, which can infest granite walls.

15. The Taurill are:
    a. poisonous to the touch
    b. a hive mind
    c. reptilian

16. Tauntauns smell worse on the _____ .

17. The fireworms of Eol Sha are also known as _____ .

18. Ysalamiri claws:
    a. are tipped with poison
    b. grow directly into the branches of Mrykr's trees
    c. are fifty centimeters long

19. TRUE OR FALSE: The Falleen have mammalian ancestry.

20. Sand People are also called _____ .

21. Clone madness:
    a. is caused by the touch of a defective clone
    b. is found in early clones that grew too quickly
    c. occurs when the Force is present in a clone

22. Hibernation sickness is characterized by:
    a. temporary blindness
    b. disorientation
    c. muscle stiffness and weakness
    d. hypersensitivity
    e. madness
    f. All of the above
    g. None of the above
    h. Some of the above, depending on severity

23. Rachuk roseola causes:
    a. a rash
    b. a strange discoloration in the eyes
    c. hiccups
    d. high fever

24. Spaarti cloning cylinders are:
    a. machines the Empire used to grow clones
    b. machines the New Republic uses to grow clones
    c. a component of cloning machines

MILITARY
AND LAW
ENFORCEMENT

MILITARY

1. TIE fighters are:
   a. long-range fighters
   b. short-range fighters
   c. long- and short-range fighters

2. Slave circuits:
   a. are on most starships
   b. allow the spaceport control tower to assist with landing
   c. allow the ship to be operated by remote control
   d. are illegal
   e. are only found on smuggling ships
   f. None of the above

3. "All we need is a ship and a rock to land it on" is the unofficial motto of _____ .

4. Corellian corvettes are nicknamed _____ .

5. Without precise calculations, a ship traveling through hyperspace could:
   a. fly right through a star
   b. bounce too close to a supernova
   c. explode

6. On an X-wing, how are the wings unfolded into the "X" position?
   a. The astromech droid must activate the fusial thrust engine.
   b. The transparisteel canopy must be down.
   c. The S-foils must be locked into attack position.

7. The T-65 X-wing is a small single-pilot starfighter also known as _____ .

8. What is "by the book" in the *Redemption* scenario?

9. What are eyeballs?

10. What are squints?

11. What are dupes?

12. What are brights?

13. AT-ATs are:
    a. Imperial guns
    b. Imperial walkers
    c. Imperial scout walkers

14. The armor on an AT-AT is:
    a. blaster resistant
    b. green
    c. nonexistent

15. The Death Star had:
    a. a superlaser powerful enough to destroy worlds
    b. a cylindrical shell
    c. illuminescences

16. An AT-AT has:
    a. heavy blaster cannons
    b. ion cannons
    c. proton torpedoes

17. The second Death Star was being built:
    a. at the Maw installation
    b. in the Endor system
    c. at Black 15

18. TRUE OR FALSE: An ion cannon obliterates electrical and computer systems.

19. The traditional weapon of a Tusken Raider is a:
    a. blaster
    b. vibroblade
    c. gaderffi stick

20. On the Death Star, the tractor beam was coupled to the main reactor in _____ locations.

21. The defense mechanism for the second Death Star was:
    a. a battery of TIE fighters

b. an internal defensive shield

c. an energy shield generated on Endor's moon

22. The traditional weapons of Ewoks are:
    a. spears and bows
    b. bows and blasters
    c. blasters and rocks
    d. sticks and stones

23. In the Battle of Endor, was the second Death Star operational?

24. TRUE OR FALSE: The Sun Crusher could wipe out entire solar systems with the touch of a button.

25. The first target of the Death Star was:
    a. Tatooine
    b. Alderaan
    c. Hoth
    d. Corellia

26. The difference between the Death Star and the Darksaber was:
    a. the shape of the shell
    b. the capacity for troop transport
    c. the competence of the designer

27. TRUE OR FALSE: The Maw Installation was closed by Grand Moff Tarkin.

28. To destroy the first Death Star, the Rebel ships used:
    a. blasters
    b. laser cannons
    c. proton torpedoes

29. A Sun Crusher could be destroyed:
    a. with a direct hit to its ion engines
    b. by dismantling its hurlothrumbic generator
    c. by sending it into a gas giant
    d. All of the above

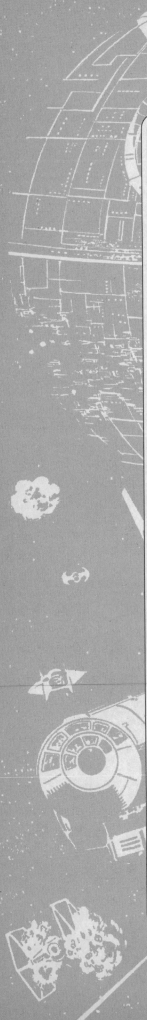

30. The Death Star was developed by:
    a. Qwi Xux
    b. Darth Vader
    c. Grand Moff Tarkin

31. TRUE OR FALSE: Sand People always ride side by side.

32. Grand Admiral Thrawn used opponents' _____ to find a way to defeat them.

33. The Alliance officer charged with the command of all Rebel ground and fleet forces on Hoth was:
    a. General Madine
    b. General Dodonna
    c. Admiral Ackbar
    d. General Rieekan

34. How did Admiral Ozzel alert the Rebels to the Imperial's presence when the squadron arrived in the Hoth system?
    a. His flagship bombarded the energy field.
    b. He came out of lightspeed too close to the system.
    c. He relayed a message to his probe droid.

35. To escape TIE fighters and a Star Destroyer in the Hoth system, Han Solo:
    a. hid with the garbage being dumped from the Star Destroyer
    b. jumped to lightspeed
    c. flew into an asteroid field

36. TRUE OR FALSE: The Rebels' plan in the Battle of Endor was to disable the shield on the moon. Once the shield was disabled, cruisers would create a perimeter while fighters would fly into the superstructure and try to knock out the main reactor.

37. Who led the starfighters in the Battle of Endor?
    a. General Calrissian
    b. General Solo
    c. Princess Leia Organa

38. How did the Rebels open the Imperial bunker door on Endor's moon?
    a. They paid for the door's computer code.
    b. Artoo-Detoo discovered the door's computer code.
    c. They blasted it open with a stolen walker.
    d. From inside a stolen walker, Han Solo asked the guards to open the door.

39. Who called the Rebel retreat in the Battle of Endor?
    a. General Calrissian
    b. General Solo
    c. Admiral Ackbar
    d. Mon Mothma

40. The commander of the Rebel forces on Yavin 4 was:
    a. Princess Leia
    b. General Dodonna
    c. Mon Mothma

41. How many Star Destroyers attacked Hoth?
    a. one
    b. six
    c. ten

42. To escape the Imperial Fleet and Admiral Needa's Star Destroyer, Han Solo:
    a. hid with the garbage being dumped from the Star Destroyer
    b. jumped to lightspeed
    c. flew into an asteroid field

43. The strike team landed on Endor's moon in:
    a. an Imperial shuttle disguised as a cargo ship, using an Imperial code
    b. a TIE fighter, using an Imperial code
    c. the *Millennium Falcon*, using a stolen Imperial code

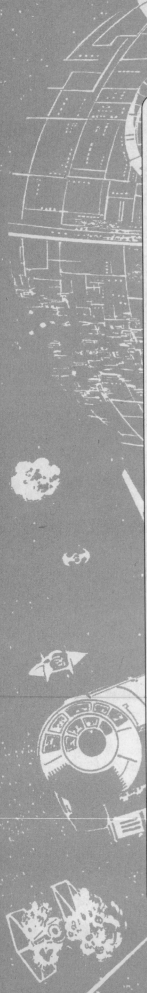

44. Who led the strike team?
    a. General Calrissian
    b. General Solo
    c. Princess Leia Organa

45. Who was the sole survivor of the Yevethan raid on Polneye?
    a. Eri Palle
    b. Plat Mallar
    c. Akanah

46. The target on the first Death Star was:
    a. the reactor
    b. a small thermal exhaust port
    c. a tiny hole left by the builders

47. When the Rebels evacuated Hoth they flew out in:
    a. X-wings, under cover of the ion cannon
    b. troop transports, with two fighters each, under cover of the ion cannon
    c. a stolen Star Destroyer, under cover of the ion cannon

48. The Battle of Endor was planned and executed from:
    a. Hoth
    b. Tatooine
    c. Coruscant
    d. Sullust
    e. Endor

49. One of the deciding factors in the Battle of Endor was/were:
    a. the fact that the second Death Star had no weapons
    b. the Ewoks
    c. Talon Karrde

50. In the Battle of Yavin, the Rebels attacked the Death Star with:
    a. 100 ships
    b. 60 ships
    c. 50 ships

d. 30 ships

e. 10 ships

51. In the Battle of Endor, Lando Calrissian broke off the fighter attacks because:

a. the Imperials had too many TIE fighters

b. the Death Star's shield was still up

c. he thought Luke Skywalker was dead

52. In the Battle of Yavin, the Imperials had to fight the Rebels ship-to-ship because:

a. the Death Star had no small weapons

b. the Rebel ships were too small to show up on Death Star screens

c. the Rebel ships flew too close to the Death Star

d. the Rebel ships were small enough to evade the turbolasers

53. Probe droids:

a. are also known as probots

b. relay their information in an Imperial code

c. are medical assistants

54. Princess Leia Organa placed the plans for the Death Star in which droid?

a. Too-Onebee

b. See-Threepio

c. Artoo-Detoo

55. The Emperor's Hand was:

a. a small spying device

b. an elite operative, with control of the Force

c. a black palm filled with information cards

56. Message droids are best used when:

a. the recipient expects a message

b. the message must be delivered fast, and you cannot risk the HoloNet and its relays

c. you have a simple message that requires a simple answer

57. Blackhole reported to:
    a. the Emperor
    b. Darth Vader
    c. Grand Admiral Thrawn

58. Whose spies discovered the location of the second Death Star?
    a. Admiral Ackbar
    b. Han Solo
    c. Borsk Fey'lya
    d. Crix Madine

59. Who was Ysanne Isard?

60. What was Saber Enterprises?

61. Which former spy for Lord Vader fled the Empire, saved Chewbacca's life on Ota, and is still at large?
    a. Mole
    b. Boba Fett
    c. Labria

LAW ENFORCEMENT

1. How do smugglers signal for help at any of the hideaways?
   a. send a signal
   b. offer to pay
   c. send a copy of the legitimate cargo manifold
   d. send a copy of the contents of the real cargo

2. What was the first settled asteroid on Smuggler's Run?
   a. Skip One
   b. Skip 52
   c. Skip 35

3. The contact on Kessel who alerted the Imperials and caused Han Solo to dump his spice shipment was:
   a. Sinewy Ana Blue

    b. Lando Calrissian

    c. Moruth Doole

4. The names of Talon Karrde's vronskrs are _____ .

5. Salla Zend:
   a. is an information broker
   b. had a base on Myrkr
   c. is considered honest
   d. refuses to have anything to do with slave running or kidnapping
   e. None of the above
   f. All of the above

6. TRUE OR FALSE: Talon Karrde never gets politically involved.

7. The Rodian Greedo worked for:
   a. Xizor
   b. Darth Vader
   c. Boba Fett
   d. Jabba the Hutt

8. Jabba the Hutt called Han Solo:
   a. a lying, cheating scum
   b. his favorite decoration
   c. a worthless spice smuggler

9. Why was Nandreeson after Lando Calrissian?
   a. Lando killed Nandreeson's brother.
   b. Lando stole from Nandreeson's private storeroom.
   c. Lando won Cloud City from Nandreeson in a sabacc game.

10. Celebrated shipjacker Evet Scy'rrep:
    a. was the basis for a series on *Galactic Bandits*
    b. knocked off fifteen starliners
    c. said he robbed luxury cruisers because that's where the credits are
    d. All of the above

11. Who killed Jabba the Hutt?
    a. Artoo Detoo
    b. Han Solo
    c. Greedo
    d. Boba Fett
    e. Leia Organa

12. Greedo was killed by:
    a. Jabba the Hutt
    b. Darth Vader
    c. Han Solo
    d. Ben Kenobi

13. Name the largest criminal organization in the galaxy under the reign of Emperor Palpatine.

14. Orko Skymine was a sham corporation put together by:
    a. Exar Kun
    b. the Hutt organization
    c. Black Sun

15. TRUE OR FALSE: After the death of Jabba the Hutt, Talon Karrde became a top operator in the galaxy's fringe community.

16. Jabba the Hutt's chief lieutenant and majordomo was:
    a. Boba Fett
    b. Ayddar Nylykerka
    c. Bib Fortuna

17. Name the eight loyal Vigos of Xizor, the Dark Prince.

18. Mara Jade is Talon Karrde's:
    a. lover
    b. hired assassin
    c. main assistant

19. Salacious Crumb was:
    a. the Emperor's Hand

b. Nandreeson's assistant

c. Jabba the Hutt's favorite pet

20. The droid in charge of cyborg relations for Jabba the Hutt was:

a. Eve-Ninedenine

b. Eve-Ninedeninetwo

c. Eve-Ninedeninethree

ANSWERS

HISTORY

EVENTS

1.	b	(1 point)
2.	a, b	(1)
3.	a	(3)
4.	a	(3)
5.	c	(1)
6.	True	(2)
7.	a, d	(2)
8.	b, d	(1)
9.	d	(1)
10.	a	(3)
11.	b	(3)
12.	a	(2)
13.	a	(3)
14.	d	(2)
15.	b	(3)
16.	c	(1)
17.	d	(2)
18.	c	(1)
19.	b	(3)
20.	b	(2)
21.	c	(2)
22.	a	(2)
23.	False	(3)
24.	c	(2)
25.	e	(2)
26.	a	(3)
27.	b	(2)
28.	True, only for Biggs to lose his life a few moments later	(2)
29.	False	(3)
30.	c	(1)
31.	b	(1)
32.	b	(1)

33. a, b   (3)
34. d   (2)
35. d   (2)
36. a, b   (2)
37. c   (3)
38. b   (3)
39. Anakin Skywalker   (1)
40. False   (2)
41. a   (2)
42. Darth Vader   (1)
43. Bossk, Zuckuss,
    Dengar, IG-88,
    Boba Fett,
    4-LOM   (6: 1 point each)
44. b   (3)
45. d   (2)
46. d   (1)
47. d   (2)
48. my master   (1)
49. b   (3)
50. c   (3)
51. True   (2)
52. a   (2)
53. b   (2)
54. True   (2)
55. d   (2)
56. False   (2)
57. False   (2)
58. c   (2)
59. c   (1)
60. False   (3)

FAMOUS QUOTES

1. Leia Organa   (1)
2. Yoda   (2)

3. Emperor Palpatine   (1)
4. Ben Kenobi   (1)
5. Emperor Palpatine   (2)
6. Jabba the Hutt   (3)
7. Yoda   (2)
8. See-Threepio   (1)
9. Admiral Ackbar   (3)
10. Darth Vader   (2)
11. Yoda   (1)
12. Han Solo   (1)
13. Ben Kenobi   (2)
14. Leia Organa   (2)
15. Yoda   (1)
16. Han Solo   (1)
17. Ben Kenobi   (2)
18. Grand Moff Tarkin   (3)
19. Darth Vader   (2)

PEOPLE

1. e   (1)
2. c   (2)
3. c   (1)
4. a   (3)
5. Yes   (2)
6. b   (3)
7. Lelila   (3)
8. a   (3)
9. c, e   (2)
10. d   (2)
11. AA-23   (2)
12. Jacen Solo, Jaina Solo,
    Anakin Solo   (3)
13. she never met him   (2)
14. b   (3)
15. False   (2)

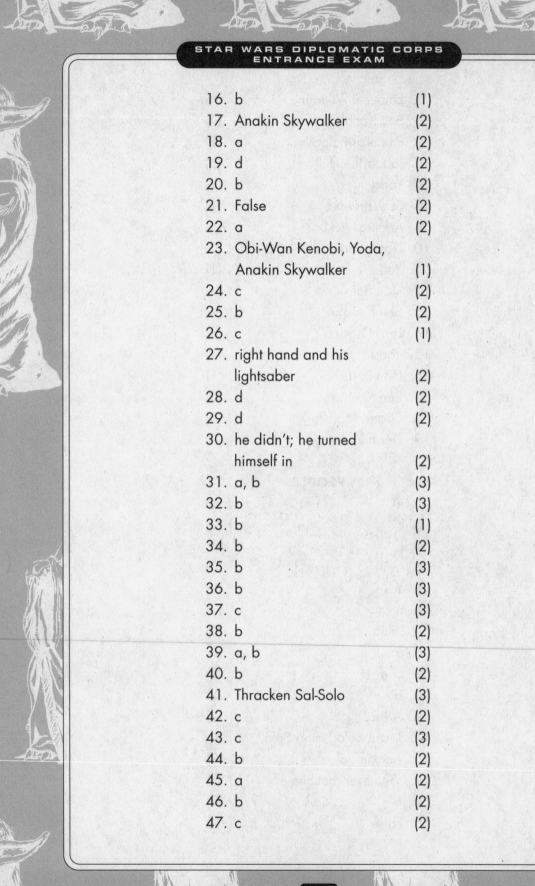

16. b   (1)
17. Anakin Skywalker   (2)
18. a   (2)
19. d   (2)
20. b   (2)
21. False   (2)
22. a   (2)
23. Obi-Wan Kenobi, Yoda,
    Anakin Skywalker   (1)
24. c   (2)
25. b   (2)
26. c   (1)
27. right hand and his
    lightsaber   (2)
28. d   (2)
29. d   (2)
30. he didn't; he turned
    himself in   (2)
31. a, b   (3)
32. b   (3)
33. b   (1)
34. b   (2)
35. b   (3)
36. b   (3)
37. c   (3)
38. b   (2)
39. a, b   (3)
40. b   (2)
41. Thracken Sal-Solo   (3)
42. c   (2)
43. c   (3)
44. b   (2)
45. a   (2)
46. b   (2)
47. c   (2)

48. a (1)
49. b (2)
50. c (1)
51. d (2)
52. a (2)
53. d (1)
54. c (2)
55. c (2)
56. a (3)
57. b (3)
58. d (1)
59. False (3)
60. a (2)
61. c (3)
62. c (1)
63. Ben Kenobi (1)
64. c (3)
65. a (2)
66. c (2)
67. a (2)
68. b (2)
69. d (2)
70. The tracks were side
    by side, and the blast
    points were too accurate (3)
71. c (2)
72. True (2)
73. c (2)
74. b (2)
75. c (2)
76. c (1)
77. b (1)
78. b (2)
79. c (3)
80. a (3)

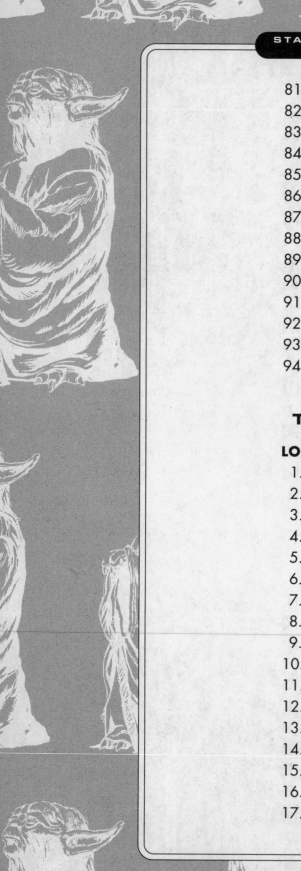

81. c	(3)
82. c	(2)
83. a	(2)
84. c	(1)
85. b	(1)
86. True	(2)
87. False	(3)
88. a	(3)
89. c	(3)
90. the Jedi Knights	(1)
91. c	(3)
92. b	(3)
93. a, b	(3)
94. d	(3)

THE JEDI KNIGHTS

LORE, THEORY, AND THE FORCE

1. True	(2)
2. True	(1)
3. False	(1)
4. True	(1)
5. False	(3)
6. True	(1)
7. b	(3)
8. b	(1)
9. b	(3)
10. an energy field	(2)
11. a, b	(2)
12. False	(1)
13. b, c, d	(2)
14. True	(1)
15. b, c, e, h	(3)
16. True	(1)
17. b	(3)

18. d   (2)
19. False   (3)
20. False   (3)
21. False   (2)
22. True   (1)
23. False   (3)
24. True   (1)

JEDI HISTORY

1. a   (3)
2. c   (3)
3. True   (3)
4. c   (3)
5. False   (1)
6. b, d   (3)
7. b   (2)
8. b   (2)
9. Yoda   (3)
10. "Pass on what you have
    learned, Luke."   (3)
11. b   (2)
12. True   (3)
13. a, d, e, f, i   (3)
14. b   (3)
15. b   (3)
16. b   (3)
17. b   (3)
18. c   (2)
19. a   (3)
20. f   (3)
21. d   (3)
22. c   (3)
23. e   (3)
24. b   (3)

INTERSTELLAR TRAVEL

ASTRONOMY AND GEOGRAPHY

1. d (2)
2. b (3)
3. a (3)
4. False (1)
5. a, c, d (3)
6. c (3)
7. h (3)
8. k (2)
9. d (3)
10. l (2)
11. b (3)
12. f (1)
13. n (3)
14. m (2)
15. p (3)
16. o (2)
17. i (3)
18. j (3)
19. q (3)
20. a (3)
21. e (1)
22. g (1)
23. s (1)
24. r (1)
25. t (3)
26. b (3)

(3 points each:)

27. a. Great Pit of Carkoon
    (Sarlacc)
   b. Western Dune Sea
   c. Jabba's palace
   d. Fort Tusken
   e. Northern Dune Sea

    f. Bestine

    g. Arnthout

    h. Mos Eisley

    i. Motesta

    j. Anchorhead

    k. Tosche Station

    l. Jundland Wastes

    m. Wayfar

28. b   (1)

29. c   (1)

30. c   (1)

TRAFFIC CONTROL AND PROTOCOLS
Ship Identification I

1. TIE interceptor   (2)
2. X-wing fighter   (1)
3. I-7 Howlrunner   (3)
4. Imperial Star Destroyer   (1)
5. A-9 Vigilance   (3)
6. CloakShape fighter   (3)
7. E-wing fighter   (3)
8. TIE fighter   (1)
9. Y-wing fighter   (2)
10. Imperial landing craft   (2)
11. Z-95 Headhunter   (3)
12. Scimitar assault bomber   (3)
13. TIE bomber   (2)
14. B-wing fighter   (2)
15. TIE/D fighter   (3)
16. Mon Calamari cruiser   (2)
17. Rebel Blockade Runner   (1)
18. TIE defender   (3)
19. Interdictor cruiser   (3)
20. *Lambda*-class shuttle   (3)

21. A-wing fighter (2)
22. Incom T-16 Skyhopper (2)

Ship Identification II

1. k (3)
2. j (3)
3. m (3)
4. n (3)
5. d (3)
6. a (2)
7. f (3)
8. g (3)
9. e, i (3)
10. l (3)
11. b (3)
12. c (3)
13. h (1)
14. o (3)
15. p (1)

SOCIOLOGY AND ANTHROPOLOGY

POLITICAL AFFILIATIONS

1. a (2)
2. a (3)
3. a (2)
4. a (3)
5. a (3)
6. b (1)
7. c (3)
8. a (3)
9. b (1)
10. a (3)
11. c (3)
12. b (1)

13. c   (2)
14. b   (3)
15. a   (3)
16. c   (3)
17. a   (3)
18. c   (3)
19. a   (3)
20. b   (1)
21. a   (3)
22. a   (3)
23. b   (3)
24. a   (3)
25. c   (3)
26. b   (3)
27. b   (3)
28. c   (1)
29. c, then a   (2)

LINGUISTICS AND LITERATURE
(3 points each:)

1. c
2. c
3. a
4. c
5. a
6. b
7. d
8. sing
9. c
10. a

SOCIAL CUSTOMS

1. a   (1)
(3 points each:)
2. a

3. Luke Skywalker
4. c
5. sabers, coins, flasks, staves
6. alive
7. c
8. fatal
9. Giant Ithorian snail
10. smell
11. sipped slowly
12. green
13. purple
14. Vader did not eat or drink in
    public

TECHNOLOGY

1. b   (1)
2. a, b, c   (2)
3. b   (3)
4. b   (3)
5. a   (1)
6. b   (3)
7. on the chest   (1)
8. True   (2)
9. False   (3)
10. c   (3)
11. a   (2)
12. b   (3)
13. False   (1)
14. a   (1)

IDENTIFY THE PARTS OF AN R2 ASTROMECH DROID

1. radar eye   (1)
2. infrared receptor   (3)
3. function indicators   (3)

4. hard data input   (2)
5. spacecraft linkage and
    repair arms   (3)
6. loudspeaker   (3)
7. system ventilation   (3)
8. power systems diagnostic
    connectors   (3)
9. recharge couplings   (3)
10. third tread   (1)
11. BTU exhaust wave   (3)
12. access panels   (2)
13. auditory sensors   (2)
14. electromagnetic field
    sensor unit   (3)
15. holographic projector   (1)
16. sensory input head   (3)
17. head rotation point   (3)
18. utility functions door   (3)
19. actuating coupler   (3)
20. power cells   (3)
21. motorized treads   (2)

BIOLOGY AND ZOOLOGY

1. a, b   (1)
2. Yavin 4   (3)
3. night   (3)
4. Hoth   (2)
5. banthas   (3)
6. energy   (1)
7. b, c   (2)
8. one thousand years   (1)
9. suction cups   (3)
10. b   (2)
11. asteroids   (1)

12. sting (3)
13. c (1)
14. rock slugs (3)
15. b (3)
16. inside (1)
17. lava dragons (3)
18. b (3)
19. False (3)
20. Tusken Raiders (1)
21. b (3)
22. h (3)
23. a (3)
24. a (2)

MILITARY AND LAW ENFORCEMENT

MILITARY

1. b (2)
2. a, b, c (3)
3. the Rogue Squadron (3)
4. Blockade Runners (3)
5. a, b (1)
6. c (2)
7. a snub fighter (3)
8. One pilot would play *fleethund* and race out to engage the first TIE flight, while the other three fighters remained in close as backup. (3)
9. TIE starfighters (3)
10. TIE interceptors (3)
11. TIE bombers (3)
12. advanced TIE models (3)
13. b (2)
14. a (2)

15.	a	(2)
16.	a	(2)
17.	b	(3)
18.	True	(3)
19.	c	(2)
20.	seven	(3)
21.	c	(1)
22.	a	(1)
23.	Yes	(1)
24.	True	(3)
25.	b	(1)
26.	a, b	(3)
27.	False	(3)
28.	c	(2)
29.	c	(3)
30.	a	(3)
31.	False	(3)
32.	art	(3)
33.	d	(2)
34.	b	(2)
35.	c	(2)
36.	True	(2)
37.	a	(2)
38.	d	(2)
39.	c	(2)
40.	b	(2)
41.	b	(2)
42.	a	(2)
43.	a	(2)
44.	b	(2)
45.	b	(3)
46.	b	(1)
47.	b	(2)
48.	d	(2)
49.	b	(2)

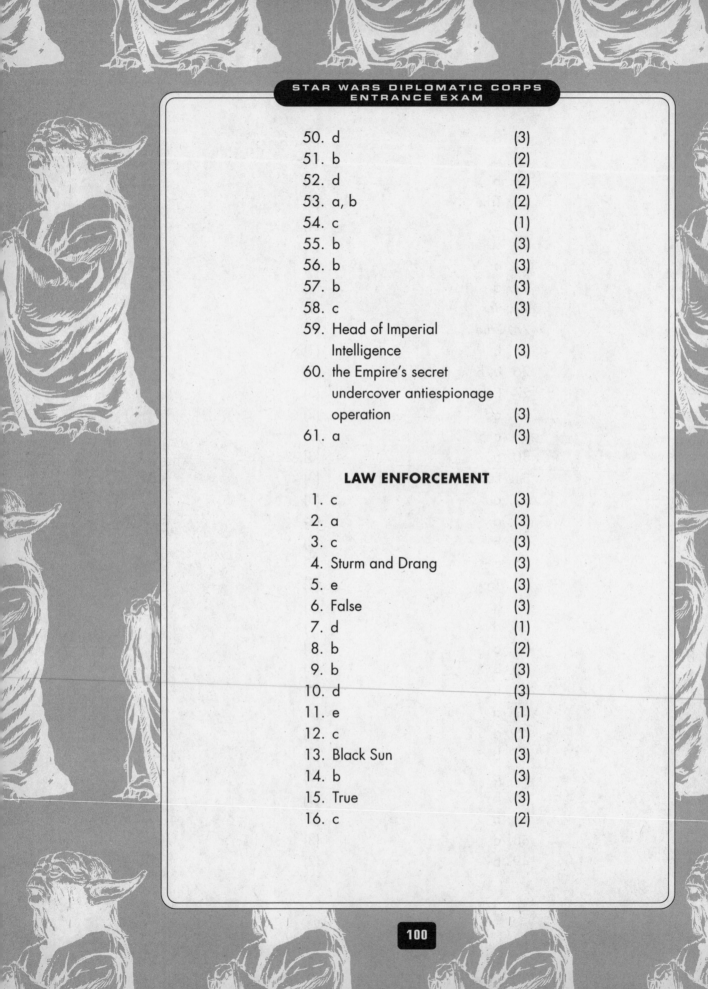

50. d   (3)
51. b   (2)
52. d   (2)
53. a, b   (2)
54. c   (1)
55. b   (3)
56. b   (3)
57. b   (3)
58. c   (3)
59. Head of Imperial
    Intelligence   (3)
60. the Empire's secret
    undercover antiespionage
    operation   (3)
61. a   (3)

LAW ENFORCEMENT

1. c   (3)
2. a   (3)
3. c   (3)
4. Sturm and Drang   (3)
5. e   (3)
6. False   (3)
7. d   (1)
8. b   (2)
9. b   (3)
10. d   (3)
11. e   (1)
12. c   (1)
13. Black Sun   (3)
14. b   (3)
15. True   (3)
16. c   (2)

17. Durga the Hutt, Kreet'ah
the Kian'thar, Clezo the
Rodian, Wumdi the Etti, Perit
the Mon Calamari, Lonay the
Twi'lek, Sprax the Nalroni,
Vekker the Quarren
(8: 1 point each)
18. c   (3)
19. c   (2)
20. a   (2)

SCORING

To determine your score, add up the point values for all of the questions you answered correctly. Using that total, consult the list of job categories below, and you will find some of the key positions for which you are most qualified. Those positions are:

POINT SPREAD   **JOB TITLE AND DESCRIPTION**

950–1145   AMBASSADOR: Stationed at consulates throughout the galaxy, this highest diplomat represents the New Republic in all its affairs.

800–949   MINISTRY COUNCIL MEMBER: Ranking just below the Ambassador, the Ministry Council Member reports directly to the New Republic Senate and helps mediate disputes and conflicts.

600–799   DIPLOMAT: Intergalactic negotiation is the art of the Diplomat who has experience and knowledge in interacting with all species.

400–599   OBSERVER: Assigned to a specific sector of space, the Observer monitors the countless worlds of the galaxy, looking for problem areas.

200–399   PROTOCOL OFFICER: The Protocol Officer advises Diplomats, Ministry Members, and the Head of State of the nuances of ceremony and etiquette followed by species throughout the galaxy.

50–199   OBSERVER ASSISTANT: The Observer Assistant helps the Observer determines what issues are worth investigating.

0–49   RESEARCH ASSISTANT: The Diplomatic Corps could not function without the able help of the Research Assistant, who provides information to all officers within the corps.

These are but a few of the jobs available within the Diplomatic Corps, designated specifically to help you in career planning and placement. For a more comprehensive list, contact the New Republic Diplomatic Corps, Office of Employment Resources, Central Administration Building, Coruscant.

Congratulations!

SOURCES

With a bit of research, reading, and viewing, you will find the answers in the materials listed below. The materials are listed by section.

HISTORY

Ambush at Corellia
Assault at Selonia
Before the Storm
Champions of the Force
Children of the Jedi
Classic Star Wars: The Early Adventures
The Courtship of Princess Leia
The Crystal Star
Dark Apprentice
Dark Empire: The Collection
Dark Empire II: The Collection
Dark Force Rising
Darksaber
The Empire Strikes Back
The Empire Strikes Back (novelization)
The Empire Strikes Back: The Screenplay
A Guide to the Star Wars Universe
Heir to the Empire
Jedi Search
Junior Jedi Knights: The Golden Globe
The Last Command
The New Rebellion
The Paradise Snare
Return of the Jedi
Return of the Jedi (novelization)
Return of the Jedi: The Screenplay
Shadows of the Empire
Shield of Lies
Showdown at Centerpoint
Star Wars

Star Wars: Droids: The Kalarba Adventures
Star Wars: The National Public Radio Dramatization
Star Wars (novelization)
Star Wars: The Screenplay
The Truce at Bakura
Young Jedi Knights: The Shadow Academy

THE JEDI KNIGHTS

Champions of the Force
Children of the Jedi
The Courtship of Princess Leia
Dark Apprentice
Dark Empire: The Collection
Dark Empire II: The Collection
Dark Force Rising
Darksaber
The Empire Strikes Back
The Empire Strikes Back (novelization)
The Empire Strikes Back: The Screenplay
A Guide to the Star Wars Universe
Heir to the Empire
Jedi Search
The Last Command
Return of the Jedi
Return of the Jedi (novelization)
Return of the Jedi: The Screenplay
Shadows of the Empire
Star Wars
Star Wars (novelization)
Star Wars: The Screenplay

INTERSTELLAR TRAVEL

Champions of the Force
Children of the Jedi
Classic Star Wars: The Early Adventures
The Courtship of Princess Leia
The Crystal Star

Dark Empire: The Collection
Dark Empire II: The Collection
Dark Force Rising
Darksaber
The Empire Strikes Back
The Empire Strikes Back (novelization)
The Empire Strikes Back: The Screenplay
A Guide to the Star Wars Universe
Heir to the Empire
Jedi Search
The Last Command
Return of the Jedi
Return of the Jedi (novelization)
Return of the Jedi: The Screenplay
Shadows of the Empire
Star Wars
Star Wars: The Essential Guide to Characters
Star Wars (novelization)
Star Wars: The Essential Guide to Vehicles and Vessels
The Star Wars Source Book
Star Wars: The Screenplay
Star Wars Technical Journal

SOCIOLOGY AND ANTHROPOLOGY

Classic Star Wars: The Early Adventures
The Courtship of Princess Leia
Dark Apprentice
Dark Empire: The Collection
Dark Empire II: The Collection
Dark Force Rising
The Empire Strikes Back
The Empire Strikes Back (novelization)
The Empire Strikes Back: The Screenplay
A Guide to the Star Wars Universe
Heir to the Empire
Jedi Search
The Last Command
Return of the Jedi

Return of the Jedi (novelization)
Return of the Jedi: The Screenplay
Shadows of the Empire
Star Wars
Star Wars (novelization)
Star Wars: The Screenplay
X-Wing: Book One: Rogue Squadron

TECHNOLOGY

Dark Apprentice
The Empire Strikes Back
The Empire Strikes Back (novelization)
The Empire Strikes Back: The Screenplay
A Guide to the Star Wars Universe
Heir to the Empire
Jedi Search
The Last Command
Return of the Jedi
Return of the Jedi (novelization)
Return of the Jedi: The Screenplay
Star Wars
Star Wars: The Essential Guide to Characters
Star Wars: The Essential Guide to Vehicles and Vessels
Star Wars (novelization)
Star Wars: The Screenplay
The Star Wars Source Book
Star Wars Technical Journal
The Truce at Bakura
X-Wing: Book One: Rogue Squadron

BIOLOGY AND ZOOLOGY

Dark Empire: The Collection
Dark Empire II: The Collection
Dark Force Rising
Darksaber
The Empire Strikes Back
The Empire Strikes Back (novelization)
The Empire Strikes Back: The Screenplay

A Guide to the Star Wars Universe
Heir to the Empire
Jedi Search
The Last Command
The New Rebellion
Return of the Jedi
Return of the Jedi (novelization)
Return of the Jedi: The Screenplay
Shadows of the Empire
Star Wars
Star Wars (novelization)
Star Wars: The Screenplay
X-Wing: Book One: Rogue Squadron

MILITARY AND LAW ENFORCEMENT

Champions of the Force
Children of the Jedi
Classic Star Wars: The Early Adventures
Dark Force Rising
Darksaber
The Empire Strikes Back
The Empire Strikes Back (novelization)
The Empire Strikes Back: The Screenplay
A Guide to the Star Wars Universe
Heir to the Empire
Jedi Search
The Last Command
The New Rebellion
Return of the Jedi
Return of the Jedi (novelization)
Return of the Jedi: The Screenplay
Shadows of the Empire
Shield of Lies
Star Wars
Star Wars (novelization)
Star Wars: The Screenplay
The Star Wars Source Book
Star Wars Technical Journal
X-Wing: Book One: Rogue Squadron

BIBLIOGRAPHY

Comic Books

Classic Star Wars: The Early Adventures 1–9, Russ Manning, Dark Horse Comics, 8/94–4/95

Dark Empire: The Collection, Tom Veitch and Cam Kennedy, Dark Horse Comics, 1995

Dark Empire II: The Collection, Tom Veitch and Cam Kennedy, Dark Horse Comics, 1995

Star Wars: Droids: The Kalarba Adventures, Dan Thorsland and Ryder Windham, Dark Horse Comics, 1995

Books

Ambush at Corellia, Roger MacBride Allen, Bantam Books, 1995

Assault at Selonia, Roger MacBride Allen, Bantam Books, 1995

Before the Storm, Michael P. Kube-McDowell, Bantam Books, 1996

Champions of the Force, Kevin J. Anderson, Bantam Books, 1994

Children of the Jedi, Barbara Hambly, Bantam Books, 1995

The Courtship of Princess Leia, Dave Wolverton, Bantam Books, 1994

The Crystal Star, Vonda N. McIntyre, Bantam Books, 1994

Dark Apprentice, Kevin J. Anderson, Bantam Books, 1994

Dark Force Rising, Timothy Zahn, Bantam Books, 1992

Darksaber, Kevin J. Anderson, Bantam Books, 1995

The Empire Strikes Back (novelization), Donald F. Glut, Del Rey Books, 1980

A Guide to the Star Wars Universe, Bill Slavicsek, Del Rey Books, 1994

Heir to the Empire, Timothy Zahn, Bantam Books, 1991

Jedi Search, Kevin J. Anderson, Bantam Books, 1994

Junior Jedi Knights: The Golden Globe, Nancy Richardson, Boulevard Books, 1995

Junior Jedi Knights: Lyric's World, Nancy Richardson, Boulevard Books, 1996

Junior Jedi Knights: Promises, Nancy Richardson, Boulevard Books, 1996

The Last Command, Timothy Zahn, Bantam Books, 1993

The New Rebellion, Kristine Kathryn Rusch, Bantam Books, 1996

The Paradise Snare, Ann Crispin, Bantam Books, 1997

Return of the Jedi (novelization), James Kahn, Del Rey Books, 1983

Shadows of the Empire, Steve Perry, Bantam Books, 1996

Shield of Lies, Michael P. Kube-McDowell, Bantam Books, 1996

Showdown at Centerpoint, Roger MacBride Allen, Bantam Books, 1995

Star Wars (novelization), George Lucas, Del Rey Books, 1976

Star Wars: The Essential Guide to Characters, Andy Mangels, Del Rey Books, 1995

Star Wars: The Essential Guide to Vehicles and Vessels, Bill Smith, Del Rey Books, 1996

The Star Wars Sourcebook, Bill Slavicsek and Curtis Smith, West End Games, 1987

Star Wars Technical Journal, Shane Johnson, Del Rey Books, 1995

The Truce at Bakura, Kathy Tyers, Bantam Books, 1994

Young Jedi Knights: Darkest Knight, Kevin J. Anderson and Rebecca Moesta, Boulevard Books, 1996

Young Jedi Knights: Heirs of the Force, Kevin J. Anderson and Rebecca Moesta, Boulevard Books, 1995

Young Jedi Knights: Jedi Under Siege, Kevin J. Anderson and Rebecca Moesta, Boulevard Books, 1996

Young Jedi Knights: Lightsabers, Kevin J. Anderson and Rebecca Moesta, Boulevard Books, 1996

Young Jedi Knights: The Lost Ones, Kevin J. Anderson and Rebecca Moesta, Boulevard Books, 1995

Young Jedi Knights: Shadow Academy, Kevin J. Anderson and Rebecca Moesta, Boulevard Books, 1995

X-Wing: Book One: Rogue Squadron, Michael A. Stackpole, Bantam Books, 1996

X-Wing: Book Two: Wedge's Gamble, Michael A. Stackpole, Bantam Books, 1996

Movies

Star Wars: A New Hope
The Empire Strikes Back
Return of the Jedi

Scripts

The Empire Strikes Back: The National Public Radio Dramatization, Brian Daley, Del Rey Books, 1995

The Empire Strikes Back: The Screenplay, Leigh Brackett and Lawrence Kasdan, story by George Lucas, O.S.P. Publishing, 1994

Return of the Jedi: The National Public Radio Dramatization, Brian Daley, Del Rey Books, 1996.

Return of the Jedi: The Screenplay, Lawrence Kasdan and George Lucas, story by George Lucas, O.S.P. Publishing, 1994

Star Wars: The National Public Radio Dramatization, Brian Daley, Del Rey Books, 1994

Star Wars: The Screenplay, George Lucas, O.S.P. Publishing, 1994

ACKNOWLEDGMENTS

I could not have done this project alone. The *Star Wars* universe is incredibly rich and diverse, and in doing this project, I haven't even scratched the surface.

But to get this far took the work of countless people. My heartfelt thanks go to Lucy Wilson for thinking of me in the first place; Sue Rostoni for providing all the material I needed and then some; and Steve Saffel for his willingness to brainstorm with an author who has more ideas than she knows what to do with.

I also need to thank the writers, artists, game designers, and nonfiction compilers who have toiled before me in this universe. I couldn't include everything in the space allowed, but I tried. Oh, I tried. If I made a mistake in or accidentally neglected your corner of the universe, please accept my apologies.

Thanks also have to go to Dean Wesley Smith for putting up with dinner discussions that began with "Did you know that the script for *Return of the Jedi* is shorter than the script for *Star Wars*?" and ended with ". . . so Threepio says to Jabba the Hutt . . ." Thanks to Julie K. Starr for going back to kindergarten for me, and thanks to the authors, particularly Ann Crispin, who took time from busy schedules to help me out. Special thanks to Kevin J. Anderson for reminding me that I am anal retentive enough to do this project. (What are old friends for, right, Kev?)

Finally, my deepest thanks go to my sister, Sandra L. Hofsommer. Every time I call her with some crazy writerly request, she digs right in. This time, she rallied her colleagues on short notice to provide sample tests, blue books, and real exams for those of us who've been out of school so long that we can't remember test format. (Yikes!) Thanks go to those teachers, all from St. Cloud, Minnesota, or the Minneapolis–St. Paul area: Catherine Carlson, Marian Day, Harlan Hewitt, and Don Hofsommer. Thanks also to my nephew, Knute Hofsommer, for so willingly giving up his study guides to his college entrance exams. Thanks also to Linnea Fredrickson of Cliff Notes for her very helpful suggestions.

I appreciate all the help, folks. I couldn't have done it without you.

ABOUT THE AUTHOR

Kristine Kathryn Rusch is an award-winning fiction writer. She has published fifteen novels under her own name: *The White Mists of Power; Afterimage* (written with Kevin J. Anderson); *Facade; Heart Readers; Traitors; Sins of the Blood, The Escape* (with Dean Wesley Smith); *The Fey: Sacrifice; The Long Night* (with Dean Wesley Smith); *Rings of Tautee* (with Dean Wesley Smith); *The Devil's Churn, Star Trek: Klingon!* (with Dean Wesley Smith); *Invasion: Soldiers of Fear* (with Dean Wesley Smith); *The Fey: Changeling; The Fey: Rival;* and *Star Wars: The New Rebellion*. Her short fiction has been nominated for the Nebula, Hugo, World Fantasy, and Stoker awards. Her novella, *The Gallery of His Dreams*, won the Locus Award for best short fiction. Her body of fiction won her the John W. Campbell Award, given in 1991 in Europe.

Until last year, Rusch edited the *Magazine of Fantasy & Science Fiction*, a prestigious fiction magazine founded in 1949. In 1994, she won the Hugo Award for her editing. She started Pulphouse Publishing with her husband, Dean Wesley Smith, and they won a World Fantasy Award for their work on that press. Rusch and Smith edited the *The SFWA Handbook: A Professional Writers Guide to Writing Professionally*, which won the Locus Award for Best Nonfiction. They have also written several novels under the pen name Sandy Schofield.

She has been a *Star Wars* fan since 7:20 P.M. on May 25, 1977.